The Last Showdown

M. Duggan

A Black Horse Western

ROBERT HALE · LONDON

© M. Duggan 2002
First published in Great Britain 2002

ISBN 0 7090 7065 9

Robert Hale Limited
Clerkenwell House
Clerkenwell Green
London EC1R 0HT

Typeset by
Derek Doyle & Associates, Liverpool.
Printed and bound in Great Britain by
Antony Rowe Limited, Wiltshire

ONE

Chomping the burnt pastry of Ma Keeley's meat pie, Jubal recalled the last time he had dined with his boyhood pal Dan Keeley. It had been a fraught occasion. As was this occasion. Jubal being a plain speaker had informed Dan and his wife that they had only themselves to blame for their troubles.

'That's easy for you to say,' Dan Keeley grumbled. 'You're not a family man.'

'And thank the Lord for that,' Jubal responded. 'And I ain't surprised Aggie ran off,' he continued determined to have his say. The truth was he felt a good deal of sympathy for Aggie Keeler, now Mrs Munn. 'You forced that girl to marry Munn.'

'We had her best interests at heart,' Ma Keeley whined.

Dan kept silent. Lowering his gaze he stared hard at his faded dungarees, unwilling to meet Jubal's hard-eyed stare. But then Jubal Strike had always been a hard man. A man who seldom smiled and said little.

Silence descended. In unspoken agreement no one mentioned that when Aggie had run away from her elderly husband she had emptied Munn's safe.

And now Munn was dead and he had left his general store and assets to his widow, providing she returned to claim them within the space of a year. In the event of her non-return the whole lot went to Munn's spinster sister Minnie.

'Don't you dare judge us, Jubal Strike,' Mrs Keeley snapped, unable to contain herself. 'Don't you be forgetting you were quite prepared to see an innocent man incarcerated for the rest of his days. Have you forgotten young Pete Smith!'

'I was a lawman,' Jubal responded patiently. 'Just doing my duty. And what in tarnation has Pete Smith got to do with this here conversation? We know for a fact Aggie ain't run off with Pete.'

Agatha had saved young Pete Smith and in the process made a fool of Jubal. But Jubal Strike was not a man to bear a grudge and he, like the girl's parents, was worried. Chewing his pie, Jubal kept his secret. Aggie had only freed young Pete Smith out of spite. She'd only done it because Jubal, being a fool, had rejected her advances.

'What Mrs Keeley means is that we all make mistakes, Jubal.' Dan looked mighty uncomfortable as well he might, for in this house Ma Keeley ruled the roost. 'Even it she were not now a woman of substance we would want her home,' Dan concluded.

'I reckon.' Jubal believed Dan.

'Carl Carpenter says Aggie is likely ruined,' Aggie's brother piped up. 'And I punched his nose and made it bleed.'

'Good for you,' Jubal observed.

'If I had a gun I would have shot him,' the youngster continued.

'Well there's no call for that,' Jubal replied. 'A

man ought only to kill to save his own hide. You just remember that or you'll find yourself either on the wrong side of the law or planted six foot under.' He paused. He saw the boy was paying scant heed. 'Talking of planting,' Jubal switched topic, 'I ain't never cared for funerals and . . .'

'You know the Perkins, Jubal, and it's only fitting you pay your last respects.' Mrs Keeley sniffed disapprovingly. 'We shall do our duty and you must do yours. And then you can get on with the business of finding Aggie.'

Jubal nodded. He had not agreed to find Aggie but he knew he could not let the matter rest.

'I'll do my damnedest,' he promised. 'But as you doubtless recall I ain't promising to haul your daughter home against her will. If the store passes to Minnie Munn then so be it.'

'All we ask is that you find our girl and inform her of her inheritance,' Dan Keeley replied. 'And if she's in trouble, well, then you get her out of it.'

Jubal wisely did not point out that Agatha Keeley could be planted six foot under. Or held in a place of ill repute. Or, even married again. Yes sir, even thinking herself still legally wedded to old Munn, Aggie was quite capable of. . . . Jubal shook his head. There was no doubt in his mind Aggie was an unpredictable female and if she wished to show her appreciation upon learning of her inheritance, why, he'd not be fool enough to turn her down a second time. He must believe she was still alive.

Jubal concentrated on the pie, unable to voice his fears because if he put his fears into words they might be true. But if anyone could find what had become of Aggie it was he.

At this moment he regretted handing in his badge. A badge gave a man authority. Folk seldom argued with a lawman and the sight of a star encouraged them to talk. But what was done was done and after he had found Aggie, well, he had his ranch waiting for him. Not to mention two female acquaintances who had shown themselves mighty obliging.

'What's the matter with your ears Jubal? They've turned bright red.' Aggie's brother piped up. To Juhal's discomfort the youngster stared hard at Jubal's ears as did everyone else at the table.

'Now you leave my ears be,' Jubal rejoined humourlessly.

'I believe Minnie Munn has hired her own man to find Aggie,' Mrs Keeley observed. She frowned at Jubal. 'Red ears guilty conscience so my pa used to say,' she snapped.

'I ain't the one at this table who should feel guilty,' Jubal protested, not liking the way she was eyeing him. 'And who is this fella you're talking about?'

She had Jubal's attention. This was a new development. One he knew nothing about, one he did not care for.

'A gentleman named Zak Bellamy,' Mrs Keeley replied sarcastically, for they all were aware Bellamy was not a gentleman.

'Goddamnit woman, why didn't you tell me sooner!' Jubal exclaimed. Young Zak was a crazy man with murderous inclinations. Zak's weapon was his blade. Jubal doubted whether Zak would be able to remember how many throats he'd cut during his progress through life.

'Now there's no call for such language at the table,' Mrs Keeley rebuked.

'And we ain't afeared Bellamy will harm our girl for he was always kind of sweet on Aggie.' Dan strove to allay Jubal's concern. 'And we have every confidence in you, Jubal. Even if Bellamy can't find Aggie we know you will succeed.' Dan spoke soothingly, fearful his wife and Jubal would soon be exchanging heated words.

'Too bad about the pastry.' Jubal allowed himself to be malicious. It was Ma Keeley's fault Aggie had scarpered. Or so he considered. 'It's just as well I'm attending the funeral. I reckon I need to speak with Minnie Munn. I need to know just what she's paid Zak to do. Bring Aggie safely back to town or maybe even slit Aggie's throat at the worst or maybe take Aggie over the border and sell her to a . . .'

'Jubal Strike, this is a respectable table!' Mrs Keeley cried. And then she burst into tears and rushed from the room.

'Minnie is a Christian woman,' Dan muttered, his expression worried. 'Besides which Zak is . . .'

'Sweet on Aggie.' Jubal shook his head. 'You're too trusting, Dan. Minnie believes the store rightly belongs to her.' Jubal paused. 'And so do I.' He snorted with disgust. 'Aggie only stayed with Munn a few weeks before taking off and the old fool has still gone and left her his property. And we can't bury our heads in the sand, Dan. There's no predicting how this matter will be resolved.' Jubal pushed away his empty plate. He'd finished the pie, burnt pastry and all. 'Well I guess I'd better go and put on my best suit. I'd not like to disgrace Mrs Keeley.'

Although he did not care to admit it Jubal was now a worried man. Clearly Zak Bellamy had a lead. Jubal, as he changed into his best suit, found himself

wondering whether he would need to kill Zak
Bellamy to safeguard Aggie's life.

Despite the oppressive heat, Mrs Keeley had
covered her face with a heavy black veil. Uncharitably
Jubal reflected that maybe Ma Keeley might not be so
eager for Aggie to return if Aggie were not now a
wealthy widow. It would be mighty convenient having
a daughter who owned the general store.

Jubal had worn his suit to keep Mrs Keeley happy.
Now he wished he had not. The material was heavy
and nowadays his jacket seemed an uncomfortable
fit. He longed to scratch but dared not. The service
would he wearisome. The parson would drone on
without flagging. And the picture painted of
Grandma Perkins would not be a true one. She
would be depicted as a saintly woman whereas in
reality the old woman had been as cantankerous as
could be.

But Jubal had liked the old woman.

Doubtless her slow-witted son Martin was glad to
be relieved of his ma's presence. Jubal thinned his
lips. In time Mrs Keeley with her nagging ways would
become another Grandma Perkins.

The old woman had shocked folk hereabouts by
declaring that Aggie had done right running off with
Munn's money and it she were in Aggie's shoes she
would have done exactly the same. After all, Munn
had only himself to blame for being fool enough to
lust after a woman young enough to be his granddaughter.

Again Jubal's ears grew red. He was old enough to
be Aggie's pa, and, goddamnit Aggie's pa was his
friend, but that did not stop him imagining a tearful,
contrite Aggie hell-bent on expressing her gratitude.

He'd be darn stupid to turn her down again and . . .

'And here we are,' Mrs Keeley observed cheerfully. Funerals were a social occasion. After the planting there'd be the funeral tea and a chance to catch up with the gossip. Not that folk would dare gossip about Agatha Munn, not whilst Mrs Keeley was around. But they would all be aware of Jubal's purpose. They would all know Dan had summoned him here to find Aggie.

Just the woman I want to see! Jubal spotted the short, perspiring ball of lard that was Minnie Munn. Miz Munn looked fit to burst out of her black dress. She also looked as though she had been sewn into her dress. She glared at Jubal as though he were the Devil himself and his presence at the funeral was an affront. From beneath black brows Jubal glared right on back at Minnie Munn and from the way she dropped her gaze he knew with certainty that Zak Bellamy had not been paid to return Agatha safely to her family.

As Jubal headed towards Minnie, she in turn headed towards the Perkins shack. She vanished inside. Undeterred Jubal, determined upon having the truth from Minnie, followed inside only to find that Minnie had escaped him via the back door.

The shack was empty apart from the parson's new wife, a girl young enough to be the parson's daughter. Jubal had heard the old wife had died in childbirth, for the parson had insisted upon producing an offspring each year despite the woman's ill health.

From a side room came the sound of hammering.

'What the hell is going on? Who is locked in?' Jubal demanded.

'Poor Clara Perkins is overcome with grief. She has

taken leave of her senses,' the parson's wife gabbled nervously and then rushed out as if afraid to be alone with Jubal.

'The hell you say!' Jubal was perplexed. The death of Clara's mother-in-law would not be enough to drive Clara mad.

'It's me. Ex-Marshal Jubal Strike,' he hollered.

Silence descended.

And then Clara's voice replied. 'Thank the Lord,' came the response. 'I've prayed for help and he has sent you, Marshal Strike. I know you won't fail me in my hour of need.'

Outside the funeral began. Minnie Munn, thankful that ex-Marshal Strike had stayed in the house, positioned herself beside the parson's wife. The woman looked nervous.

Martin Perkins removed his hat and gripped the brim tightly.

Doc, who had not thought to bring his bag, could do nothing for Clara. Doc glared at the parson. Parson Blane had actually offered to hold an exorcism after the funeral in order to drive out the demons which he maintained were now residing in Clara. Parson Blane was a great believer in demons.

'Goddamnit,' Doc had declared, 'I've lost count of the times I've cut into folk and I ain't never seen a demon residing in one of them. We must differ on this matter, Parson. All Clara needs is a sleeping-draught.'

Blane however was still determined to drive out demons. He would have his way in this matter, he had maintained.

Respectfully the old woman's coffin was lowered into the grave. Someone belched and the parson, looking ready to breathe fire, opened his Bible. And, at that very moment gunshots were heard from inside the house.

Mrs Keeley gripped her husband's arm. It had to be Jubal. Jubal was bound to disgrace them. Mrs Keeley had heard Clara had been locked away for her own good and Jubal must have taken exception. The man was a meddler.

'Lord, he's shot the lock.' Doc also knew Jubal Strike.

Jubal, his expression grim, emerged from the shack and headed towards the funeral party with Clara Perkins in his wake, her hair in disarray and her gown torn, for she had put up a fight to prevent them locking her in.

There was no doubt in his mind as to what had to be done.

'You ought not to have let her out, Marshal Strike, you ought not,' Martin Perkins cried out. 'Grief has driven her crazy. She just can't help herself.'

'There ain't nothing wrong with this woman,' Jubal bellowed. 'And she don't need no exorcism. She needs heeding.' Angrily Jubal elbowed his way through the mourners. He planted himself beside the grave and looked down at the coffin. 'What we've got to do is open it up,' he announced, as though there was no doubt in his mind that it would be done.

'Are you mad, Strike! Grandma Perkins is dead,' Doc exclaimed angrily. 'And poor Clara is out of her mind. Temporarily that is. As is only natural. She'll recover, I can assure you.'

'There's a demon inside her. And I shall cast it out. The abomination will return from whence it came,'

Blane yelled, his eyes glinting with a fanatical light which Jubal recognized as trouble.

Jubal ignored the parson. 'Get down there, Dan, and prise off the lid.'

'You'll do no such thing.' Mrs Keeley gripped Dan's arm. She glared at Jubal. 'Are you mad!'

'That old woman might be alive. We've got to make sure,' Jubal declared, surprised to see folk were beginning to distance themselves from him.

Mrs Perkins stared wildly at her husband. 'Varmint!' she cried. 'You put her in alive.'

'Now, Mother, that ain't so,' Martin Perkins soothed. 'Calm yourself or Doc here might just have to certify you.'

'I'm lawman around here.' The sheriff, who had been keeping at the back of the mourners stepped forward. 'And I say there ain't no need to disturb the dead. Doc's word is good enough for me. Besides which you have no jurisdiction here, Strike. You're an ex-lawman ain't you? You gave up your badge.'

'That's as may be,' Jubal rejoined. 'But we all make mistakes. Even Doc,' he concluded pointedly. 'We must satisfy ourselves the woman is dead before we plant her.' He regarded the sea of faces around him, faces which were looking increasingly hostile and decidedly unsympathetic. 'We're decent folk, every one of us, and I am sure—'

'To open the coffin would be an act of indecency.' Doc was not of a mind to be persuaded.

'How so?' Jubal had run out of patience.

'Martin laid her out without a stitch to cover her,' Clara Perkins cried. 'He said she did not need anything.'

'Enough of this unseemly talk.' The parson clearly

intended to exercise his authority. 'Proceed with the burial,' he commanded.

To his astonishment the command was ignored. Folk continued to move away from Jubal Strike the parson noted. Even their sheriff looked mighty uneasy.

'Open that goddamn coffin,' Jubal roared, his control snapping. 'Get down there Dan and get that goddamn lid lifted or I'll know the reason why. And if anyone thinks different they had best be prepared to haul iron.'

Doc faced Jubal, his face red with anger. 'You're loco Jubal,' he declared. 'The woman is dead. I saw her myself before Martin laid her to rest.' He eyed Martin with disfavour. 'The poor soul was decently covered at that time.'

'Well I ain't convinced.' A hefty shove from Jubal sent Doc sprawling. Doc had never looked at the body. 'Get to it Dan!'

Dan Keeley clambered down beside the coffin. He kept his lips buttoned for he could see Jubal was ready to explode with rage. Most times Strike was a reasonable and mild-mannered *hombre* but there were times when Jubal erupted like a volcano.

'It's got to be done,' Dan announced. 'There ain't no help for it.' He coughed. 'Now that the matter has been raised we must all satisfy ourselves the poor soul has passed away.'

'And ain't scrabbling at the lid trying to dig herself out,' Jubal observed harshly. 'Get on with it Dan.' As he was speaking his hand reached for his .45. 'Anyone who interferes will answer to me,' he warned.

Ignoring the uproar occasioned by the sight of

Jubal's drawn .45, Dan took up a shovel. Grandma Perkins's box was nothing more than something Martin had cobbled together out of packing-cases. The flimsy lid was soon prised free.

'Blasphemy,' the parson clasped his hands as if to pray. A foul stench emanated from the box. But Dan doing what had to be done, knelt and peered inside whilst Jubal kept the mourners in his sights. From the corner of his eye, to his astonishment Jubal observed Mrs Keeley practically hopping with rage.

'You've shamed us all, Jubal Strike,' she cried hysterically, clearly unable to control her emotions.

'My God!' Dan hollered, 'she's got one eye open and I can tell you now it's got a glint in it. That ain't the eye of a dead person. You get down here Doc and see for yourself.'

Pandemonium broke out. Minnie Munn gave way to hysterics and started to screech that maybe Munn had not been dead after all.

'Goddamnit woman, he had a heart attack,' Doc hollered shoving Minnie to one side before squatting down beside Grandma Perkins's grave.

'Goddamnit, she's breathing.'

To Jubal's disgust the parson, sinking to his knees, began to pray loudly. The name Lazarus was mentioned. Jubal resisted an urge to kick the man. If it had been left to the parson nothing would have been done. They'd probably be shovelling earth right now.

Jubal bolstered his Peacemaker. He glared at the sheriff. 'I can see you ain't one to uphold the law without fear or favour,' he observed.

'What the hell do you mean by that, Strike?' the younger man blustered.

'I mean that a decent lawman can't trouble himself with keeping the good opinion of other folk. Nor can he worry about making a fool of himself.'

To Jubal's disgust Minnie Munn was being carried inside. He knew he would not be able to get any sense out of her now. He had lost his opportunity to question the woman. But he guessed he knew exactly what Zak Bellamy had been hired to do. Her face had betrayed her.

'You pass on a message to Minnie Munn.' Jubal glared at the fresh-faced sheriff. 'You tell that woman that if Agatha Keeley meets with harm I'll be heading back this way. And I ain't a man to leave vengeance to the Lord.'

'Now what are you talking about, Strike?' the sheriff rejoined.

Jubal thinned his lips, 'Zak Bellamy is poison. He also carries a sharp blade.'

'Lord, Strike, I wish someone would slit your goddamn throat, for you are nothing but trouble. Zak does not intend to slit Aggie's throat. His intentions may well be dishonourable but they ain't lethal.' The sheriff shook his head in disgust. 'I ain't a fool, Strike. Minnie Munn has wasted her money. That polecat has a mind of his own and he ain't got a mind to slit Aggie's throat! And another thing, Strike, you ain't a lawman now. You're retired. This is my town.'

Jubal spat. 'Then open your eyes. See them folk milling. I see trouble.'

Jubal turned away. The young sheriff was right. The old days were gone. He had no regrets. He had his ranch. That is, he would have his ranch once he had found Aggie. And he had to admit that leaving the running of the ranch to his two hired men was not something he was happy about. But he must forget about his ranch until he had found Aggie.

'You've done right Jubal.' Dan patted him soundly on the back. 'You've done right,' he reiterated. 'Who would have thought it! She was almost buried alive.'

'And I reckon she would not have been the first,' Jubal observed sourly. 'And I ain't convinced Martin did not know the truth of it. But either way he'll pay. Old Ma Perkins will make his life hell.' Jubal paused. 'If she lives.'

'If she lives,' Dan reiterated. 'But no, Jubal, what you say – that can't be!' Dan was clearly aghast.

Jubal shrugged. 'We'll never know, Dan. We'll never know.'

The two men were alone now, for old Grandma Perkins, hastily wrapped in a sheet, had been carried inside. Folk milled around outside the Perkins home and loud was the condemnation of Martin Perkins.

'Get along home folks. Get along home or I'll be forced to fill up my jailhouse. Whether she pulls through is in the hands of the Lord.' The sheriff was finally endeavouring to take control.

'And Parson Blane,' someone yelled.

'Goddamnit, get along home those of you who have no business here.' Once again Jubal hauled out his .45.

Folk began to move.

'What's gotten into you Jubal?' Dan was clearly puzzled.

'Folk are mighty riled and riled folk turn mean,' Jubal explained. 'I know from experience.' He shrugged. 'Once a lawman always a lawman, I guess. In any event I feel obliged to safeguard Perkins's miserable hide.'

Dan nodded. 'They've taken heed Jubal. They've taken heed.'

Jubal grinned unpleasantly. 'I've always said the Peacemaker was rightly named.'

The young lawman had also drawn his weapon. Maybe the angry talk had persuaded him to take a more forceful hand.

Folk were leaving and the risk of violence was passing. Martin Perkins was safe for now. Jubal saw he wasn't needed here.

'Well, I'd best get moving myself. I'll do all that I can to find Aggie,' he pledged. 'I'm headed for Bartlett. That's where I hope to learn more. Sam the stagecoach driver clearly remembers that Aggie disembarked in Bartlett. But what the hell she did next is anyone's guess.' Jubal shook his head. 'Even if I find her, Dan, she'll not come back to the farm. Aggie's tasted independence now . . .'

'Just find her, Jubal. Find my girl.' Dan wiped away a tear. 'I ought never to have listened to Mrs Keeley.'

'Amen to that.' Despite the seriousness of his mission Jubal grinned. Dan Keeley would not change. And it was at times such as this that Jubal was mighty glad he'd never had a hankering for matrimony.

But, to his shame, he had a hankering for Miz Aggie.

He mounted up.

'The Lord will reward you,' Mrs Keeley called out.

Jubal's ears grew red. It was not the Lord whom he wanted to reward him.

TWO

Munn had been an old fool. A wise man would not have married a smart woman young enough to be his granddaughter. Aggie, knowing her parents would send Jubal to find her, would have done her utmost not to leave a trail for him to follow.

As he headed for Bartlett Jubal considered various possibilities. Knowing Aggie he knew she would do the unexpected but he still believed he would be able to find her. And he was sure she would he glad to see him when he told her she was now a rich woman. Indeed he was counting on it.

By the time he arrived in Bartlett Jubal was dust-covered, weary and hungry but nevertheless he made Sheriff Flock's office his first stop.

Flock was a big man, calm of manner and with eyes deceptively mild. Jubal had already wired the sheriff to inform Flock of his purpose. Now he introduced himself and then reiterated that as a friend of the family he felt it his duty to assure himself that Aggie was alive and well.

Flock nodded. 'Seems to me,' he observed slowly, 'that this girl's family are looking to obtain free provisions, seeing she now owns a sizeable store.' Flock's eyes grew speculative. 'If the girl had a rich husband what was she doing in my town?' He paused. 'And has it occurred to you Strike, she may not wish to return home even if you hunt her down. I'd let sleeping dogs lie if I were you. You'll save yourself a deal of trouble. You have a ranch now, so I hear.'

Jubal nodded.

'And your nearest neighbour is Jake Day,' Flock continued.

'So I believe.'

'Yes sir. I know Jake Day and a mighty ambitious *hombre* he is. I heard tell he is looking to expand his spread.'

Jubal stifled an oath. He understood the veiled warning. With an almighty effort he returned to the matter in hand.

'I've no intention of hauling Aggie home against her will,' he reassured Flock. He thinned his lips. 'And it would be a very unusual woman who'd willingly walk away from a considerable inheritance.' One that she did not deserve, he thought, but kept those thoughts to himself.

'As I wired you she ain't in town,' Flock declared. 'I've searched. As you requested. Thoroughly,' he concluded. He shook his head. 'By the time I received your wire Mrs Munn had upped and left us. And with good reason. That little lady is a thief!'

Jubal kept silent. Flock could not be referring to the money Aggie had taken from Munn.

'She's a mighty fine-looking young woman,' Flock continued. He shook his head. 'But she's a thief. As I told you she was here a short while and then she was gone. How, I don't know. She did not book passage on any stage out of town.' Flock paused. 'The fact of the matter is, this young lady stayed a while with the Widow Wagg before taking off. She'd paid in advance, naturally. After she'd left the widow discovered her engagement ring was missing. And a pearl necklace. Seems she had a habit of hanging them on the mirror hook.'

Jubal stayed silent. His first instinct had been to defend Aggie, but . . .

'Yes sir,' Flock continued, 'I scoured the town. I even searched Harlots' Row just outside of town in case she'd—'

'Now hold your horses,' Jubal exclaimed hotly. 'We're talking about a respectable woman.'

'They were all respectable at one time or another,' Flock rejoined. 'But in any event she was not there. I checked out the livery stables and Mrs Munn did not buy a horse.' Flock shrugged. 'She must have met someone. I'd say Mrs Munn has found herself a new man.' Flock paused, 'There's a *hombre* called Bellamy in town. He's also looking for Aggie Munn. I told him I could not help him. Know him, do you?'

Jubal nodded.

'He's still hanging around,' Flock continued. 'Either he ain't in that much of a hurry to find the girl or he does not know where to start looking.'

Again Jubal nodded. He waited for Flock's verdict on Bellamy.

'He's an odd sort of fellow,' Flock mused. 'It's almost as though he is two people, confident braggart and jester one moment. And then the next moment that young man behaves as though he is liable to jump at his own shadow. I'd say that *hombre* has problems.'

'He's dangerous,' Jubal stated quietly. 'Make no

mistake about it. Zak Bellamy can be lethal. He's a natural killer. He favours a blade.'

Flock snorted with disgust. 'Give me a bullet every time,' he declared. 'What do you say, Strike?'

'My weapon has always been the .45,' Jubal rejoined. He shrugged. 'But to defend myself I'd use whatever means came to hand.' He paused. 'I ain't as handy as Bellamy when it comes to using a blade,' he concluded. 'Cutting throats ain't my style.' He did not add that Zak's practice was to jump his targets. More than one body found in an alleyway could be attributed to Zak.

'So what do you aim to do?' Flock queried. He hesitated. 'If I were you I'd see to my ranch and leave the rest of it.'

Jubal shook his head. 'I must play the cards as they fall. I'll start by asking around.' He winked. 'You've given me an idea.'

'What idea?'

Jubal grinned. 'I'm keeping my thoughts to myself. Right now, I need a long hot soak. A tub is a good place to think matters through, so I've found. And then I aim to have a decent meal.'

Jubal paused at the door. His expression hardened. 'If any harm has befallen Aggie someone is going to pay,' he vowed.

Flock stared long and hard at the closed door. He happened to know Jake Day had put in a bid for what was now Jubal Strike's spread. No doubt about it, Strike was making one hell of a mistake searching for Miz Aggie when more urgent matters needed attention. But Strike, Flock reckoned, would find that out for himself.

Heading for the bath-house, Jubal felt uneasy. He

had a hunch that finding Aggie would not be an easy task. And the longer this took the more cause he would have to worry about what this Jake Day might be planning. His was a small spread hemmed in by large, powerful, long-established ranches. The owner, an old-timer moving East to die in his daughter's house, had sold the ranch to Jubal by way of repaying a favour. There'd been far better offers.

'Now don't you be thanking me,' the oldster had advised with a cackle.

Jubal understood the situation he was now in. Jake Day had his eye on Jubal's ranch. And, damnit, he ought to be there. His two hired men were hard-working and trustworthy but it wasn't their place to handle the kind of trouble that only a Peacemaker could settle. Jubal's life savings had bought the ranch and goddamnit, no way was anyone going to take it from him. He was a fool. He had no business looking for Aggie.

He could curse himself a hundred times but he knew he was driven to satisfy himself she was safe and well.

And sure as hell that did not mean that he was carrying a torch for the young hussy.

'Cheer up, mister,' encouraged the bath-house owner, a very much overweight *hombre*.

'I want a full tub and make damn sure I get hot water,' Jubal advised. He scowled. On the opposite side of Main Street lounging against a hitching post was Zak Bellamy. And Zak, catching Jubal's eye, actually winked.

Jubal ignored young Zak. Clearly Zak had run out of steam. Zak hadn't the damnedest idea where to head next. North, south, east or west, Zak had no idea which direction Aggie had taken.

The hapless youngster who'd been sent to fill the tub slapped water over the floor. And then bolted.

Jubal climbed into the tub. He was expecting Zak. Sure as hell Zak's voice beyond the curtain heralded his arrival. Jubal waited, relaxing in steaming water. His hand beneath the harsh towel held his .45. Mirthlessly he smiled as he recalled how a fellow lawman he'd once known had been blasted in the midriff whilst relaxing in a tub.

'Get out of my way, you barrel of lard,' a voice yelled and then the curtain was jerked aside. Zak looked peaceable enough but Jubal wasn't fooled. Zak had been ready to set about the proprietor. Zak was an unpredictable polecat!

'They do say,' Zak smirked, 'That bright-red ears signify a guilty conscience. You've taken your time, Jubal. Lord knows what might have befallen Aggie!'

'How would you know about consciences,' Jubal rejoined easily, 'seeing as you ain't got one? And what's your intention concerning Miz Agatha? Just what have you been hired to do?'

'I don't mean to harm her.' Zak's manner changed dramatically. Now he evinced fear. Jubal wasn't fooled by Zak's pretence of fear. And then abruptly Zak grinned confidently. 'Old Miz Munn wants her planted. Naturally I ain't going to do it.'

Jubal studied the younger man. Zak was attempting to grow a moustache and a miserable attempt it was. In Jubal's opinion Zak wasn't right in the head.

'Then why are you looking for Aggie?' Jubal demanded.

'Now don't get riled, Strike.' Zak now sounded fearful again. And then he was grinning, manner changing yet once more. 'You ain't that smart are you. Can't you figure it out? Lord, I've been sweet on Aggie for years.' He waited expectantly. Jubal did not take umbrage. Jubal knew darn well Zak deliberately provoked confrontation.

'Well I don't reckon Aggie is sweet on you,' Jubal rejoined at last.

'How would you know? You're old enough to be Aggie's pa,' Zak snapped, clearly displeased. 'I aim to see Aggie gets that store. She deserves it. Her folk had no right forcing her to marry Munn,' Zak continued. 'Lord! Old Munn must have looked a sight on his wedding night. What do you say, Strike?'

Jubal sighed wearily. Hell, he could foresee the future. Until he found Aggie he would have this lunatic dogging his footsteps.

'I say that ain't your concern, Zak. And if you can live to my age you'll have done real well.' Jubal shook his head. 'And you ought to know better than to barge into a bath-house. Right now there is a .45 pointed at your midriff. A man of nervous disposition would have blasted you the moment you came in. Lucky for you, ain't it, that I ain't got a nervous disposition? Now are we agreed we'll work together to find Aggie?'

'Yep.' Zak nodded.

'Then I'm calling the shots,' Jubal declared.

'I intend to ride along with you,' Zak rejoined aggressively. 'But as for taking orders—'

'If you've got an idea let's hear it,' Jubal interrupted.

Zak remained silent, confirmation that he was clean out of ideas.

'I take it you've searched this town,' Jubal essayed.

'Yep.'

'Including Harlots' Row?'

'Damn you, Strike! If you're suggesting—'

'I ain't suggesting, Zak, merely pointing out that maybe Miz Aggie could be held against her will in one of those shacks.'

'Lord. I ain't thought of that,' Zak declared. He sounded real concerned.

'Well you go search whilst I finish up here and get a bite to eat,' Jubal ordered. 'And if you're riding with me Zak, try and be just the one person will you? Quit switching characters!'

'I don't know what the hell you mean.'

'I think you do,' Jubal corrected. 'And you'll do as I say. Or goddamnit I'll blast you here and now just for the hell of it. You're the last person I'd choose as a partner.'

There was a long pause. Anger glinted in Zak's eyes but he controlled himself.

'I'll go conduct a search,' Zak replied. He clenched his jaw. A sure sign he did not care to take orders.

After Zak's departure Jubal was able to relax. Aggie was a badly behaved young puss and Jubal was pretty sure she would have taken a walk to Harlots' Row purely to gawp at the unfortunate females forced to ply their profession along the Row. But she would not have gone as Mrs Munn, respectable young wife, like not she would have gone dressed as a boy. Jubal did not believe she was being held prisoner but doubtless, if this was so, Zak would find her. And searching kept Zak out of Jubal's hair.

His bath concluded, wearing clean duds, Jubal strolled to a nearby eating-house. He ate a leisurely meal and all the while he thought about Aggie and how she might have gotten out of town without being seen. Had she gone willingly with a *hombre* she'd met or had she been taken against her will?

Once again Jubal experienced a frisson of unease. Finding Aggie should have been a straightforward matter. He had a hunch it would not be straightforward at all. He guessed a twisted trail lay ahead of him.

Jubal had long since finished his apple pie when Zak entered the restaurant.

'Not a sign of Aggie!' Zak announced. 'I've scoured the Row from end to end and near got blasted once or twice. Shame on you Strike, Miz Aggie would not set foot in such a place.'

Jubal sighed wearily. 'You just ain't that well acquainted with Aggie. The Row is just the sort of place she'd want to take a peek at. Aggie's got her freedom now and she'll do just what she wants to do.'

'How'd you mean?'

'I mean there's no pa or husband around telling her what to do. She can do what she damn well pleases and I reckon she would have wanted to see the Row after dark when trade picked up.' Jubal stood up. 'What I'm doing Zak, is putting myself in Miz Aggie's shoes . . .'

Zak Bellamy hooted with laughter. 'You're loco, Strike. Even you can see your feet are too damn big to fit Miz Aggie's boots.'

'I aim to check the place out myself.'

'If you can do better, Strike, I'll eat my hat.'

'You don't have a hat!'

Jubal, with Zak in tow, headed for the outskirts of town. He smelt the Row before he reached it, for an open sewer ran the length of the place. The shacks dotting either side of the Row were in bad repair and a pig or two rooted amongst the garbage. Flock, so Jubal had heard, had cleaned up the town and driven the ladies of the line to take up residence on the outskirts where they'd be hidden from the eyes of respectable females.

'She'd never risk her good name by coming here.' Zak sounded shocked. 'Miz Aggie is a decent woman. Need I remind you?'

Jubal glowered at Zak. Decent or not Aggie was a darn thief. A sly little baggage who was causing him trouble and when he found her. . . .

'We'll see,' Jubal rejoined. He withdrew a hastily done sketch from his inner pocket. He'd made the drawing whilst eating. It was a sketch of a fresh-faced, slim young fellow. He'd seen Aggie wearing her brother's clothes before. She'd done so to scandalize them all. Ma Keeley, Jubal remembered with a grin, had boxed Aggie's ears and screeched loud enough to hurt Jubal's ears.

Jubal went methodically from shack to shack. He hammered loudly and announced himself as Marshal Jubal Strike, no matter that he had now handed in his badge.

Reluctantly, painted and weary faces studied his sketch. Jubal made damn sure they all took a good long look. He did not allow himself and his sketch to be dismissed out of hand. It was not until he had reached the last shack of the Row that painted nails closed over the sketch. The woman nodded and reached for the bills held in Jubal's free hand.

'He was here,' she said. 'Hanging around gawking. I cussed him plenty but the varmint refused to budge.' She paused. 'I ain't seen him for a while. I reckon he's moved on.'

'Any idea where?'

'I ain't got a clue.'

'Is there anything else you can tell us? I'd be grateful.'

'How grateful?'

'Well that depends on what you've got to say,' Jubal encouraged.

She winked at Jubal. 'That depends on what you've got in your wallet.'

'Wallet be damned. You damn floozie . . .' Zak started forward, meaning to shake the information out of the woman.

Jubal moved sharply. Stepping into Zak's path he brought his elbow sharply back, the bone connecting with Zak's midriff.

'You bastard, Strike.' Zak staggered back reaching for his knife as he tried to regain his balance.

Jubal kicked out. His boot connected with Zak's wrist just as the knife was about to be pulled.

Zak yelled with pain but even so he lunged at Jubal. Then the two of them were down fighting in the dirt and filth of Harlots' Row, oblivious to all else.

Women came out from the shacks to scream and hoot but it was the sound of the shot that caused Jubal and Zak instinctively to break. An urge to self-preservation brought them both to their feet.

'Hell, you two look to be in a sorry state,' Flock observed. He had not come alone. Two deputies were with him, and one held the shotgun which had been fired.

'I want you out of my town, Strike,' Flock declared

without preamble. 'You're trouble. You don't mean to be but you are.'

'What the hell are you talking about!' Jubal growled.

'Nothing personal, Strike, but I've just received word that the Cash brothers have been released. I'd say the jailbirds will be looking for you, Strike. I don't want you here when they find you. I don't want no truck with the Cash brothers.'

Jubal took a deep breath. He wiped his mouth. Blood stained his knuckles.

'Goddamn you, Strike, I can't see out of my eye,' Zak Bellamy whined.

'When the Cash brothers are around innocent folk die,' Flock stated. 'They ain't normal, Strike. They ought to have been hung.'

Jubal nodded. He'd always reckoned the judge had been bribed. Not that handing out a life sentence would save the judge. Fifteen long years the Cash brothers had served and they would have counted every day. And now it seemed they had bought their way out again with a governor's pardon.

The woman had watched the fracas impassively. Jubal saw now that she was still waiting. Only money interested her.

'Let me see that.' Flock took the sketch. He grinned widely. 'I'll be damned!'

'Tell me what you know.' Jubal handed the woman a further wad of bills.

'Miz Aggie dressed as a boy,' Zak muttered in disbelief, as he too stared at Jubal's sketch. But then his thoughts returned to the Cash brothers. 'I've always admired those two galoots.' Zak smirked. 'You've reason to worry, Jubal. Real good reason.

How do you like the idea of being basted and then roasted slow on a spit?'

'Quit yapping.' The woman eyed Zak with distaste before giving her attention to Jubal. 'All I can tell you,' she said, rapidly concealing the money beneath a none too clean yellow skirt, 'Is that the young feller seemed mighty interested in a customer he identified as Ruben Goodheart. The boy kept asking questions as to what Goodheart had been getting up to.' She snorted with disgust. 'I just had to throw a pail of slops over the young jasper.'

Jubal's lips twitched. He could imagine the scene.

'I heard shouting and yelling one night,' the woman continued. 'And I'd swear it was Goodheart. But as I was otherwise engaged I never came out to see.' She paused. 'And that was the last the Row saw of Goodheart. He must have left town.' She shook her head 'The boy must have high-tailed it. I ain't spotted him hereabouts again.'

'And where can I find this Ruben Goodheart?' Jubal enquired, wondering whether Goodheart was a local rancher.

'Ruben Goodheart is the mayor of Purewater.' The woman laughed and shaking her head she sauntered back inside her shack, wide hips swaying.

'From what I've heard Purewater ain't a place I'd want to visit. Goodheart, as well as being mayor, is some kind of hell-fire preacher.' Flock shook his head in disgust. 'And all the while the *hombre* was visiting the Row.'

Jubal narrowed his eyes. 'That's where we're headed, Zak. Purewater. We've been given a lead. Maybe Goodheart can shed light on Aggie's whereabouts.' Jubal vaguely recalled Dan Keeley mentioning a boyhood pal called Ruben.

'You don't seem concerned about the Cash brothers,' observed the sheriff. 'They'll run you down.' Evidently the Cash brothers were uppermost in Flock's mind.

Jubal shrugged. 'Well, Sheriff, so long as it ain't in your town you need not worry. Let them. To hell with the Cash brothers. I've got more important matters to think about.' He eyed Zak. 'If you ride with me, maybe you'll meet your heroes. If the Cash brothers find you riding with me they'll be after your hide. Those two are bad medicine. I reckon they are criminal lunatics, and . . .' Jubal shook his head. Zak was not paying heed.

'Hell, Strike,' Zak declared self-importantly. 'You don't know me. I'd always put Miz Aggie before my own safety and—'

'So we'll head for Purewater, then.'

'I'm kind of partial to pigs,' Zak declared as he eyed the rooting creatures. There was a faraway look in his eyes. 'My old man kept them. I'd just be getting fond of a critter when he'd declare it was time to turn it into pork.' There was an odd expression on Zak's face. 'My old man met with an accident.'

'What kind of an accident?' Flock enquired.

'The pigs ate him.'

Flock swore softly. 'You'd best be riding, Strike.' He eyed Zak with disgust.

'There ain't no need for Jubal to worry.' Zak drew a finger across his throat. 'He's safe with me until we find Aggie.'

Jubal shrugged. 'I'd best set you right, Zak. You ain't in the same league as the Cash brothers. You've a way to go.'

The two glared at one another.

Flock cleared his throat. 'It's a long haul between here and Purewater. I've a hunch that only one of you will make it. But in any event, now you're satisfied Miz Aggie ain't here there's no reason for either one of you to stay.'

Jubal nodded. 'I'll be riding out tomorrow. My horse needs resting and so do I.'

'Which proves you are way past your best,' Zak smirked.

Flock would not meet Jubal's eye. He'd panicked at the thought of the Cash brothers heading his way and both he and Jubal knew it!

THREE

'Tell me about the Cash brothers,' Zak demanded eagerly. There was a glint in his eye that Jubal did not care for.

'Well there ain't much to tell except they're as bad as you've heard,' Jubal rejoined. Sidney and Thomas Cash were evil men.

'I'll see you skewered and roasted, Jubal Strike!' Sid Cash had screamed in fury. He had not been joking!

'You're a fool,' Tom Cash had stated coldly and quietly. 'You could have been a rich man. Now all you are going to be is roast meat.' Both brothers had laughed heartily.

'They tried to bribe me,' Jubal elaborated.

'And you turned them down? You damn fool!' Zak sneered. 'You should have shot them,' he winked, 'after taking their money. You could have made out they were attempting to escape,' Zak continued cheerfully. He laughed, 'Sure as hell, were they planted they would not be troubling you now. You don't fool me, Strike. You're worried plenty.'

'I was a lawman!' Jubal replied calmly. 'And I ain't worried.'

'No, of course you ain't,' Zak agreed, his tone implying otherwise.

'Slow your pace, damnit!' Jubal snapped. 'I aim to reach Purewater. That ain't possible if we run our horses into the ground.'

'She ain't in Purewater,' Zak persisted. 'You're guessing, Strike.'

Jubal nodded. 'So, I'm guessing!' he agreed. He shrugged. 'Perhaps Ruben Goodheart can shed light on Aggie's whereabouts. All I know is that Goodheart is the only lead we've got.'

Zak swore violently and then proceeded to describe what he aimed to do to Goodheart, if Goodheart had harmed a hair of Aggie's head.

Jubal allowed Zak's rage to subside. 'We must check out Goodheart and Purewater before we seek elsewhere. Now if you've got a better idea, Zak, let's hear it.'

Zak remained silent.

'And we will check out Osborne,' Jubal decided. 'It's the nearest town to Purewater after all. We may learn something.'

Zak spat. 'Or we may learn nothing at all.'

As Jubal had anticipated, during the ride to Osborne Zak gabbed plenty about the Cash brothers.

Jubal held his peace. He felt an urge to throttle Zak. He needed no reminder that the Cash brothers were out and about and aiming to get him. Zak was a pain in the butt and he was mightily relieved when Osborne came into sight.

'We'll ask,' Jubal declared, 'if anyone knows Ruben Goodheart. We'll start with the lawman.' Jubal paused. 'Ruben Goodheart interests me.'

Zak snorted. 'Goddamn Goodheart. It's Aggie we must concern ourselves with.'

'She recognized Goodheart,' Jubal observed. He held his peace. If Aggie had tried her hand at blackmailing Goodheart anything might have happened. 'We'll show Aggie's picture around. Goddamnit, it's all we can do. I'm out of ideas!'

'You're worried about her, ain't you?' Zak observed shrewdly.

Jubal shrugged. 'I reckon,' he admitted.

'I believe you'll be glad of my skills before this is over,' Zak remarked modestly.

'Your skills! You young scumbag! The only skill you've got, is blood-letting!' Jubal exclaimed in disgust.

'Well that's what I mean,' Zak smirked. 'You ain't a young man, Strike, an' maybe you ain't in the same league as the Cash brothers yourself.' Zak abruptly fell silent, 'Hell!' he exclaimed. 'I do declare we're in time for a hanging. Now ain't that something.'

'You sonofabitch,' Jubal muttered, squinting at the newly erected scaffold. The rope, he observed, was already in place. Jubal also noted that the drop wasn't near enough the right length, nor was there a trapdoor. An unlucky *hombre* was due to strangle slowly with his toes an inch or two above the boards, and everyone would be able to watch. Jubal snorted with disgust at this slipshod arrangement. If he were in charge he'd have them tear down the damn scaffold and then set matters to rights. He'd have them put in a trapdoor. He would not have folk witnessing such a spectacle. Hell, a hanging was no picnic and the devil take folk who thought it was.

'I aim to make sure I get a ringside seat,' Zak declared, seemingly oblivious to Jubal's views on public hangings.

'Such things ain't entertainment,' Jubal admonished. 'Now let's go see the sheriff.'

'What in tarnation has got into you?' Reluctantly Zak followed in Jubal's wake.

Jubal hammered on the jailhouse door.

'Whoever is out there, you can go to hell,' a muffled voice yelled in response. 'This here is my day of rest. Yes sir, even a lawman deserves a day off.'

Reaching into his back pocket, Jubal took out his tin star. He pinned it on, knowing the badge would get him inside.

'It's Marshal Jubal Strike who wants a word,' he hollered.

The door did not open immediately but open it did. A bewhiskered face with bloodshot eyes stared out. Jubal breathed in whiskey fumes.

'Strike, huh? I heard you retired.'

'You heard wrong,' Jubal lied. 'I merely considered the matter.' He laughed loudly. 'Once a lawman always a lawman.'

'What brings you to Osborne, Strike?' The lawman took Jubal's words at face value. 'I'm Fox, Sheriff Fox,' he introduced himself.

'Well I ain't exactly here on official business.' Jubal decided to stick to the truth. 'I'd be obliged if you could tell me what you know of Ruben Goodheart. Maybe he's been in town recently together with a young woman named Aggie.'

'Ruben Goodheart,' Fox muttered darkly. 'That crazy loon!' He laughed. 'Goodheart heads a crazy religious sect. Those crazy folk keep to themselves, which is how we like it.'

'So he ain't here?' Jubal essayed.

'Nope. Now if you'll excuse me—'

'Have you seen this woman?' Jubal thrust a sketch of Aggie before Fox's uninterested eyes.

'Nope,' Fox replied succinctly. He paused. 'Stay around and watch the hanging, why don't you. We're holding it come Sunday morning after service. It ought to be some sight. Yes sir, hanging is too good for that *hombre*. Hell, at the least he deserves to be burnt at the stake. Want to see him?'

'No!' Jubal rejoined.

'Don't you want to know what he's done,' Fox queried, clearly anxious to tell them the tale.

'You've made me mighty curious.' Zak spoke up loudly. 'I'm with the marshal. He can vouch for me.'

'You come on in and take a look, young fellow,' Fox offered pointedly ignoring Jubal's sour expression.

Jubal held his tongue. He knew Fox's kind. The lawman was a drunkard and a sluggard who sat on his butt while the town ran itself. And what in tarnation, Jubal asked himself, was so special about this particular prisoner? Reluctantly he followed Fox and Zak inside. He wanted no part of this. He sensed he was being dragged into something he'd best keep out of. He hung back, unwilling to enter the cell area.

'Looks like you've been having yourself a party, Sheriff!' Zak guffawed.

'You could say that,' Fox rejoined.

At that, Jubal decided he'd best take a look. He shoved Zak and Fox out of his way. And ignored Zak's protests.

'Goddamnit, Fox, you ought to be ashamed of

yourself!' Jubal rounded on Fox. The prisoner had been badly beaten and as Jubal stared at the puffed-up, disfigured, face recognition dawned. 'What in tarnation . . .' Jubal began angrily.

'Hold your horses, Strike,' Fox exclaimed, his tone sur!y. 'Now don't you be getting sanctimonious. This louse only got his just deserts. He's a woman-killer. And not just the one. This is the sixth one to be strangled and gutted and other things besides.'

Zak whistled.

'The town has been losing them one each year,' Fox explained. He coughed. 'Ladies of the line, so we kept it kind of quiet seeing as it did not concern decent folk. But this last time we caught the scumbag.'

'In the act?' Jubal essayed.

'Bending over the body. And he was covered in blood. It was on his duds, on his hands, his face, on his hair. And he'd been seen with her earlier. He lured her out back into an alley and then set to work.'

'So every year for the last six years this *hombre* has been sneaking into your town, murdering a woman and sneaking out.'

'You've said it,' Fox agreed.

Jubal snorted with disgust. 'I think not. This man's a horse-thief.'

Fox laughed. 'Ain't no one here interested in horses, Strike. We're talking about women being carved and gutted.'

'This man is a horse-thief,' Jubal reiterated. 'He ain't no woman-killer. You've tried and convicted the wrong man.'

'I bet my boots we don't lose one next year,' Fox retorted grimly.

'You're coming up for re-election ain't you?' Jubal hazarded shrewdly. 'And now you've got the killer you're certain to be re-elected.'

'Get off your high horse, Strike. You ain't never been a real lawman. All you ever did was ferry prisoners to the penitentiary. You ain't never put your hide on the line or faced down a natural born killer.'

'And that's a fact,' Zak sniggered. He was siding with Fox.

'I bought my horse off that *hombre*,' Jubal stated grimly. 'O'Banion keeps on the move and never visits the same town twice.'

'You had dealings with a horse-thief. What kind of lawman are you, Strike?' Fox demanded self righteously.

Jubal bit back an angry response. 'Hanging O'Banion would be a miscarriage of justice.'

Jubal frowned. A thought had abruptly occurred to him.

'How long has this here community of Goodheart's been around?' he asked.

Zak swore. He guessed he had an idea what was in Strike's mind.

'Maybe seven or eight years,' Fox replied after a moment's thought.

'And the killings have been going on for six!'

'Purewater folk keep away from Osborne,' Fox snorted. 'I've no reason to suspect Ruben Goodheart if that's what you are thinking. It has been a mighty long while since he showed his nose in this town.'

'Let's get out of here, Jubal.' Zak took Jubal's arm. 'We ain't got no business with this O'Banion.' Zak hustled Jubal outside. 'Miss Aggie is the one we've got to be thinking about.'

'I can't see O'Banion lynched for something he did not do,' Jubal retorted angrily shaking away Zak's hand. 'Leave me be. This ain't right.'

'We can leave town! You don't need to stay around and watch him hang.'

Jubal sighed. Words would be wasted on Zak. 'Check us in to the hotel. And get the horses into the livery.'

'And what will you be doing?' Zak asked.

'I aim to question O'Banion,' Jubal rejoined.

'We're here to help Aggie. We ain't here to save the hide of a goddamn horse-thief.'

'I said I aim to question O'Banion. Now get out of my way.'

'You're loco, Strike.' Zak moved aside.

Fox, who had been about to light up his pipe muttered an oath when Strike hammered at the door once again.

'You don't need to involve yourself, Strike,' Fox growled, but he saw his words had fallen on deaf ears.

'You don't give a damn about Miz Aggie,' Zak yelled as Jubal disappeared into the jail.

'Now that ain't so,' Jubal muttered. He eyed Sheriff Fox with disfavour. 'I'm talking with O'Banion, now, this very moment. Get out of my way.'

'More fool you, Strike, more fool you,' Fox muttered. With O'Banion convicted and hanged his job was indeed safe. 'And I'll you tell you something, Strike, something you ought to know. Folk may ride into Purewater but they don't ride out.'

'Why are you telling me this'

Fox shrugged. 'You're a lawman, same as me. I see

you mean to go to Purewater. I'm telling you traffic into Purewater is one way.' He paused. 'You have ten minutes to speak with O'Banion. This is my jail. Don't you be forgetting it.'

'That ain't likely,' Jubal rejoined, relieved that Fox was not going to make a rumpus about his speaking with O'Banion. Fox had managed to save face and that was all that counted with Fox. Wisely Jubal did not enquire why Fox had not ridden to Purewater and satisfied himself as to what was going on in that crazy place.

'Jubal Strike,' O'Banion croaked as Jubal entered the cell.

'Yep. I see you are in a sorry state.'

'Ten minutes, no longer,' Fox growled. Muttering under his breath he stomped out.

'I'm innocent. Leastways of murder. Don't let them hang me, Strike. I ain't never been in this two-bit town before. When the fifth one was killed, why I was stealing horses down Mexico way.'

'That's plausible.' Jubal scratched his chin. He reached a decision. 'I'll do my darnedest to see this town misses out on its entertainment. Now tell me how it came about. How it was you came to be beside the body?'

'Clara.' O'Banion's voice broke. 'Her name was Clara and she was a mighty fine woman.'

Jubal left the jail and headed straight for the bath-house. He needed to calm himself. What O'Banion had related had set Jubal's stomach churning. In his present frame of mind he lacked the patience to deal with wearisome Zak Bellamy. That is, in a peaceable way!

Jubal sank into the hot tub. There was no doubt in

his mind. He was duty bound to run down this multiple killer.

Ruben Goodheart, his mind told him. It had to be Goodheart. But he must go to Purewater with an open mind. Instinct was not enough. He needed evidence.

The problem was Zak. Zak would not be concerned with hunting down a killer. Zak's only concern was Aggie.

Jubal swore softly. Had Aggie crossed paths with this deranged killer? Jubal experienced real fear. Goddamnit, he cared about Aggie. And not in a fatherly way.

'You can have them for six dollars,' a familiar-sounding voice boomed. 'Real fancy they are with coloured tops red and blue. And decorated with silver stars. You'll never see a finer pair of boots. And there's a Stetson going for five dollars and new pants your size for six.'

'And the shirt?' the bath-attendant enquired.

'Hell, that's ruined. He was blasted after all!'

There was a lengthy silence before the bath attendant spoke. 'You've got yourself a deal.'

'Abilene, you come on in here,' Jubal yelled. He recognized that voice. Abilene was one crazy son of a bitch. However, Jubal did not believe Abilene was the killer.

'The curtain was pulled aside and Jubal found himself confronted with the enormous round belly of Abilene. Abilene had put on considerable weight since Jubal had last seen him.

'Hell!' Abilene yelled. Round button eyes regarded Jubal.

'Remember me do you?' Jubal enquired.

The eyes brightened. 'I do declare it's Jubal Strike.'

Jubal had been a much younger man last time he had seen Abilene. By profession Abilene was an undertaker and coffin-maker. He was also a money-grabbing son of a bitch. And something else besides.

'The damn fool has got carried away,' old Sheriff Coombs had told young Jubal. 'But it ain't as though he's harmed 'em seeing as they were dead already. So I aim to run him out of town and you keep your lip buttoned.'

Indeed Abilene had got carried away, Jubal reflected. The lunatic had tried to mummify two of his charges and the fact that certain organs must of necessity be removed had not deterred the eager undertaker.

'So you're undertaking here in Osborne?' Jubal essayed.

'Yep,' Abilene rejoined warily, recalling the last occasion he had seen Strike. 'It weren't me that done for those womenfolk,' Abilene declared. 'I've been here in Osborne but four years. Two of them were slaughtered before I ever set eyes on this two-bit town.'

'Fair enough.' Jubal nodded. 'You owe me, Abilene,' he stated bluntly.

'How so?' Abilene challenged.

'I turned a blind eye to your pursuits.'

'Now that's enough of that kind of talk.'

'I'll call in at the parlour. We need to talk privately.'

Abilene's smile had faded. 'I'm a well-respected man in this town,' he declared. 'Way back, when I did what I did I was as drunk as a skunk and out of my mind.'

'You've always known what you were doing.' Jubal smiled grimly. 'And as for you being a well-respected man, well I wouldn't have it any other way. I'll call round.'

'Suit yourself,' Abilene replied sourly.

'I intend to,' Jubal rejoined.

Jake Day was in his prime. He was a handsome man and a confident man. Hands clasped behind his back, he eyed his ramrod with disfavour.

'You're an old woman, Able,' he declared.

'I've heard tell of Strike,' Able rejoined. 'He's a hard man.'

Jake smiled. 'Strike ain't here. No one seems to know where Strike is. He's taken off. Maybe permanently.' He shrugged. 'And that's precisely what his hired hands are going to do after I've given them a talking to.'

'I don't like it boss.'

'You ain't paid to like things, Able. Now quit yapping. Get my horse.'

'Yes sir.' Able knew there was no arguing with his boss. There would be hell to pay when Strike arrived and found his two hired men had been beaten and driven off, his stock scattered far and wide and his ranch house burnt to the ground. Able shook his head. Once he'd seen Strike face down a Lynch mob. Strike hadn't given an inch.

Jubal faced Abilene across the laying-out table.

'I ain't doing it,' Abilene declared.

'And I tell you, you ain't got a choice,' Jubal replied bluntly. 'As I told you, O'Banion ain't the killer. It's a set-up. Fox needs to keep his job.' Jubal shrugged. 'I could never understand why old Sheriff Coombs let you get away with it. Ancient Egyptians my . . .'

Abilene eyed his boots. 'It weren't the sheriff who found out. 'Twas his daughter Elisa.'

'What!'

'You don't know nothing Strike. Way back then I was a deal lighter and better looking.'

'I reckon,' Jubal agreed doubtfully.

'And the sheriff's daughter was one plain woman.'

'What are you saying?'

'I'm saying I had to marry Elisa Coombs to save my hide.' Abilene smiled. 'I tell you Strike a man can live to a hundred and never know what a woman is capable of. Old Coombs was glad to see the back of her. Ain't no other way he would have turned a blind eye to my,' here Abilene coughed, 'misdeed,' he concluded lamely.

'So where is she?' Jubal demanded. He needed to know what had become of Elisa Coombs.

Abilene laughed. 'Alive and well and back at the house. You are welcome to call in to check if you have a mind.' He paused 'It weren't right, the way those killings were covered up. Folk have only just learned the extent of the horror. Fox and the town council conspired to keep it quiet. I could have lost Elisa.'

'So you'll do as I ask?'

Abilene nodded. 'I ain't got a choice.' He shook his head. 'Hell Strike, I never figured you for a lawbreaker. You must be sure of O'Banion's innocence.'

Jubal shrugged. 'I am. Fox ain't left me a choice. O'Banion swears he was blubbing over the body on account of being sweet on the victim. I believe him.'

Abilene nodded. 'It could be so. Fox knows he's got the wrong man but his job is on the line. And if you're tied in with this Strike, your life will be on the line. You'll be a wanted man for the rest of your days.'

Jubal reached into his pocket. 'As I recall Abilene, you have a mighty fine memory. Have you seen this young woman around town? And what about Ruben Goodheart? What can you tell me?'

Abilene studied Aggie's likeness. He shook his head. 'I don't reckon she's been through Osborne. As for Goodheart, he's one crazy loon but it is two years back since he visited Osborne. And the murder did not take place during his visit.' Abilene shrugged, 'Goodheart's wife and daughter are in town right now. They come in to collect medical supplies. Seems the daughter has a weak heart. And the mother, why I reckon the old bat just likes to get out of Purewater.' He shook his head, 'You had best keep your wits about you. Purewater stinks!'

FOUR

The problem was going to be Zak. Zak Bellamy would not be interested in saving the life of an innocent man, nor in hunting down a crazed killer of women. Zak was a scumbag. He could not be expected to behave decently.

Squaring his shoulders, Jubal entered the hotel. Zak had booked them both in so all Jubal had to do was collect the key. Upstairs he found Zak studying his reflection in the cracked wall-mirror.

'There's some fine-looking women at the saloon,' Zak observed slyly. 'But maybe you're too long in the tooth for such enjoyment.'

Jubal shrugged. 'I reckon you're right, Zak. But don't let me stop you from enjoying yourself. You go right ahead. But leave your money belt in the hotel safe. Those fine-looking women have light fingers.'

Zak grinned. 'I'd pay for you. But it would be a waste of good money.'

'I've got other things on my mind. This two-bit town is set to hang an innocent man. Fox won't admit he's sat on his butt and done nothing about hunting down this here deranged killer. I'm

49

convinced O'Banion is an innocent man. I've got to save his hide.'

'Hell, you are in a bad way!' Zak exclaimed. 'We're here to find Aggie. Ain't nothing else here that's our concern. If you are troubled the answer is simple. Quit town before the hanging.'

'O'Banion ain't going to hang. You're not listening.'

'I'm listening. And I don't like what I'm hearing. O'Banion is a two-bit horse-thief. He'll hang sooner or later. You're a fool, Jubal Strike. O'Banion would not risk his neck for you.' Zak shook his head. 'Now I'm heading for the saloon. You take a nap, old-timer. Tomorrow we're heading for Purewater. We'll take that town apart. And if Aggie ain't there we'll light a fire beneath Ruben Goodheart's toes. That'll get him talking. We'll find Aggie. And if Goodheart has harmed her we'll burn him to a crisp.'

'Suppose Goodheart doesn't know Aggie's whereabouts?'

'You're the one that said Goodheart is the only lead we have.'

'I wasn't thinking of torture. I won't have it!'

'We want answers, Strike. Hell, you ain't the man you used to be. See you around.' The door slammed behind Zak.

'You louse,' Jubal muttered beneath his breath. He was in his prime. Why, the widow Smith and Prudence Gator the schoolmarm could vouch for for him. Not that he would ever mention such matters to a living soul.

Jubal crossed to the window. He stared down at the street below. He watched Zak enter the bath-house. Jubal was still staring down at the street when much later Zak emerged and swaggered confidently towards the nearest saloon.

The saloon was called the High Stepper. There was a wooden figure of a dancer outside the place, toe pointed skyward, blue garter revealed.

Fox drank nightly in the High Stepper. Abilene had volunteered the information. Jubal lay down and took his nap. He was glad Zak was out of the way. It made life easier.

Darkness had fallen before Jubal awoke. He stretched slowly, smiling in the darkness of the room. His bones weren't creaking yet. And as for Zak, why no doubt that young hound-dog would be as drunk as a skunk which suited Jubal just fine.

Jubal left the hotel by way of its back entrance. He emerged into the darkened alleyway. The smell of garbage assailed his nostrils.

The town was dark save for the light spilling from the saloons. Keeping to the shadows, shoulders hunched, head bowed, Jubal headed for Abilene's funeral parlour. He thought of the women who had been murdered in this town. Beneath his breath he cussed the incompetent Fox. And then it hit him. Fox had been downright afraid to go to Purewater in search of a killer.

From Main Street a voice yelled out cheerfully, 'Hey there Fox, you mind you keep that sumbitch alive. How long do you reckon he'll last?'

'Long enough,' Fox rejoined.

'The longer the better,' came the reply. 'Hell, some of the womenfolk are planning to hurl rocks whilst he's dangling. What do you say?'

'Then maybe we ought to make sure his boots just touch the boards,' Fox rejoined. 'That ought to keep him dancing a mite longer.'

'You do that, Fox. You do that,' the unknown citizen encouraged.

'Goddamn scum!' Jubal exclaimed. Fox was not fit to be a lawman.

Abilene was waiting. 'Have you the money?' he asked without preamble.

'Yep.' Jubal stared at Abilene's workbench. There was a partly eaten cheese-and-potato pie. There was a book and there was also a row of objects.

Jubal picked up the book. Abilene, he saw, was watching carefully.

'Well I reckon I know what to expect from you,' Jubal thinned his lips. 'You ain't right in the head Abilene. You just ain't right at all. And neither is the *hombre* who wrote this goddamn book.' The explorer who had written of his travels amongst head-hunting heathens had described the process of head shrinking in detail. 'And I'm warning you, if O'Banion's head ends up in your collection I'll gut you like a fish.' Jubal glared at Abilene.

'O'Banion will receive the best of care. You're paying me to keep him safe. We have a deal. You can trust me. I keep my word.'

'I reckon,' Jubal agreed reluctantly as he counted out a wad of bills.

Abilene pocketed the money with alacrity.

'Do you reckon the murdered women put up a fight?' Jubal enquired.

'Nope. I'd say they were taken by surprise,' Abilene responded after a moment's thought. 'Whoever done it was not drunk at the time. He was cold sober and skilled in butchery.'

Jubal nodded.

'Well, I had best get my exhibits out of sight. Fox will tear this town apart,' Abilene observed sourly, 'And the Lord help us both, Jubal Strike, if folk tie us in with O'Banion's disappearance.'

'Lord help you if your exhibits are discovered,' Jubal observed. He shook his head. 'They'd ship you off to the asylum so fast your feet would not hit the ground. That's if you were lucky. Lord, those folk would stomp you into the ground if they but realized what they was harbouring.'

'And this town would tear you to pieces if they knew what you were about,' Abilene rejoined.

Jubal tapped the butt of his Peacemaker. He did not speak. It was not necessary.

'Well, ain't you got nothing to say?' Abilene demanded.

'Nope.'

'I ain't done wrong. They was all loners without loved ones to mourn 'em.'

'Then it's lucky for you, ain't it, that no one thought to check the coffins before they were planted.' Jubal scratched his head, 'You are two short, I see.' He eyed the empty jars.

Abilene laughed. 'Don't fret yourself none, Jubal, I ain't of a mind to preserve you, even though I'll be risking plenty to help out,' Abilene rejoined after a moment's thought. 'Now what else is troubling you, Strike? Spit it out. There's more on your mind than O'Banion.'

'I ain't got eyes in the back of my head,' Jubal answered. 'I've Miz Aggie to find and a crazy murdering screwball to uncover and, as I understand the situation, there is a big shot rancher with his eyes on my ranch.' Jubal paused. 'And the young sonofabitch

I'm riding with is more than likely to turn on me. Zak Bellamy can't be trusted. No way. He's a killer. Worse than that he likes killing.'

'You're a man with problems, I see.' Abilene grinned 'Problems of your own making, Strike.'

'What!'

'Well, first of all, Miz Aggie ain't your concern. She's a free woman and if she wants to up and run that is her business. Secondly, running down this here killer ain't your concern. You've turned in your badge. And if you ain't happy about your travelling companion you ought to see he meets up with an accident. That only leaves this here big-shot rancher. You're a fair shot Jubal. Why not try your hand at bushwhacking!'

'You villain!'

'I'll help out, Jubal. But not for peanuts. And not because of threats neither. I want an IOU. And if you can't meet that IOU I want a small share of your ranch. You and I go back a long way Strike. We understand one another. I'm sick of undertaking. So why not be a ranching man?'

'I ain't a fool Abilene.'

'Lord Strike, these men were dead before I took their heads!' Abilene exclaimed angrily. 'I ain't no murderer. And my hide is worth a share of your ranch. You can trust me. I won't double-cross you. I don't want your goddamn head in my collection. And as a future pard I'll tell you now, stay out of Purewater. Yes sir, pilgrims pass through town heading for Purewater and that's the last this town sees of 'em. I reckon it's mighty hard to get out of the town of Purewater. Now what do you say, Strike? Do we have a deal? Will you shake on it?'

Jubal regarded Abilene's hand with distaste. And then he remembered O'Banion, railroaded for a crime he did not commit just so Fox could keep his job. And no one gave a damn that an innocent man had been railroaded and the true murdering thug was free to kill again.

Jubal hesitated. He recognized the fact that he had to pay extra. Abilene was one odd son of a bitch and it would be dangerous to cross him. Jubal held out his hand. 'Shake,' he said. 'I don't reckon to have you as a partner but I am a man of my word. If I can't pay up in time then a partner you'll be. O'Banion ain't worth it. But I can't watch an innocent man rope-dance.' He paused. 'It's got to be tonight!'

Abilene nodded. He shook Jubal's hand. 'I reckon,' he agreed.

Sheriff Fox bellied up to the bar, his eyes fixed on the pink reclining nude whose image had been captured on canvas.

Zak Bellamy was also eyeing the painting. Zak in Fox's opinion was as drunk as a skunk. This evening Bellamy had spent freely. In Fox's opinion Strike and Bellamy were ill-matched travelling companions. Purewater was welcome to the both of them. Fox wanted them out of his town. He had a hunch Jubal Strike was going to cause a problem concerning the hanging. It was a well-known fact that Strike was as obstinate as a mule. And maybe as stupid as a mule.

Fox guessed he'd find out just how stupid Jubal was.

'Yes sir,' Zak bellowed at the bartender, 'I am telling you that Sid and Tom Cash are on Jubal's trail.

They aim to cook his hide. And between you and me Jubal is getting long in the tooth. He's past his prime. Why, it would not surprise me if I didn't have to handle the varmints myself.' Zak drew his knife and ran his finger lightly along the blade.

'Well, you've time to stay for the hanging, I reckon,' the bartender rejoined.

'You can bet your boots we'll be around. Well, maybe not Jubal. I reckon he'll be feeling kind of queasy. But I'll be there. You can count on it. And then we're heading for Purewater.'

Fox heaved a sigh of relief.

'So Sheriff, just what do you aim to do if another poor creature turns up murdered?' a hard-faced woman demanded.

'Now then Dora, don't you be concerning yourself,' Fox soothed. 'We have the son of a bitch. Tomorrow he's going to dance.'

Dora gave a snort of disgust. 'So you say. But I ain't convinced. I'm leaving this town. And the rest of the girls are going too. And this town is gonna demand your badge.'

Commotion broke out inside the saloon. Dora had been overheard. Folk began yelling at Fox demanding what he was going to do if the women wanted to leave.

'You all get out of my goddamn way.' Fox headed unsteadily towards the batwings. Without O'Banion he'd be out of a job. And he could always put the blame on the town council. And the folk who'd convicted O'Banion. The law was the law and had to be upheld. Even that obstinate cuss Strike could not argue with that. O'Banion had been tried and found guilty. He was going to dance.

From an alleyway Jubal watched as Fox lurched along the street. Jubal had removed his boots. He wanted to move quickly and silently. He was not over-confident. There was always something that could go wrong. And in that event his conscience would not allow him to harm Fox. Fox might be a polecat but he was a fellow lawman.

Jubal held his breath. His eyes swung to the batwings. At any time another drunk could come stumbling out.

Fox fumbled with his jailhouse key.

Approaching noiselessly from behind, Jubal stepped forward and clamped the chloroform-soaked pad over Fox's mouth and nostrils. Fox struggled briefly and violently but Jubal was far stronger. Fox slumped to the ground the key slipping from his hand.

Perspiration dotted Jubal's brow and shirt. He took up the key. And suddenly it hit him. He knew now how those unfortunate cruelly murdered females had been rendered helpless. Chloroform!

Jubal unlocked the jailhouse door and dragged an insensible Fox inside.

Back inside the saloon Zak Bellamy eventually passed out. His head hit the table with a thump. It was saloon policy to leave any drunken bum where he fell, so Zak was left.

Dora sauntered to the batwings, a mug of coffee in her hand. She eyed the trestle tables with disgust. It was beyond belief that pies were to be sold and consumed whilst a man breathed his last. An inno-cent man in Dora's opinion.

There was no sign of Strike, the lawman said to be opposed to the hanging. For an instant Dora found herself wondering whether she ought to warn the lawman Strike.

Sure as hell, Strike's 'pard', Bellamy, had shot his mouth off yesterday evening. And Simon, everyone's friendly bartender, aimed to cash in on Strike's misfortune. Simon aimed to contact the Cash brothers and let them know, for a price, where Strike might be found. Simon aimed to point the pair in the right direction.

'I never did trust that creep Simon.' Dora had muttered to herself. She decided against warning Strike.

'Looks like it's gonna be a fine day,' Jade joined Dora at the batwings. She winked, 'The question is whether Jubal Strike is fool enough to take on this town.'

Dora shook her head. 'You'll find Strike is no better than the rest of the men. And where the hell is Fox? It ain't like him not to be out and about acknowledging folk's congratulations.'

Jade laughed, 'Nursing a sore head, I reckon. Him and the rest of the bums in this town.'

Within the saloon Zak Bellamy was coming around. A groan left his lips. He raised his head with an almighty effort. Hammers pounded away at the top of his skull. He looked around with bloodshot eyes. Apart from a few unappetizing-looking women the saloon was empty.

And he needed to relieve himself. Uttering a louder groan and a curse Zak lurched to his feet and moved unsteadily towards the batwings.

'Get out of the goddamn way.' He elbowed the two

floozies aside and staggered out into daylight. Zak shook his head. The world was spinning. Nevertheless he managed to steer himself to the nearest alleyway.

'And to think I went upstairs with that drunken bum,' Jade moaned. She winked at Dora. 'And what a hell of a waste of time it was. That little squirt kept right on mumbling about a Miz Aggie. You don't hold a candle to Miz Aggie, he said. And then he refused to pay up.' Jade snorted. 'We'll see who has the last laugh.'

Dora gripped her friend's arm. 'What the hell are you trying to do? Get yourself killed? There's only one thing a man values more than himself and that's his money. Jade what have you done!'

Zak Bellamy fastened his pants. His hands moved to his waist. Which did not feel right. Zak's heart seemed to stop. A string of obscenities left his lips. His goddamn money belt was gone. He'd spent plenty but there'd still be a good amount left.

'No goddamn whore cheats Zak Bellamy,' he hollered. Spittle flecked his lips. Right now Zak Bellamy was one hell of a crazed man.

The two floozies at the batwings stepped aside when they saw him coming. Zak ignored them. He knew which one had done it. He'd showed her his money. And then he must have passed out. 'You thieving bitch,' he roared heading straight towards the frightened young girl.

Women screamed. But not the two at the batwings.

Zak grabbed the girl by the neck and shook her violently. 'Where the hell is my belt?' For good measure he whacked her head against the bar.

Zak Bellamy never saw who killed him. The shot

from the derringer took off the back of his head.

Jade blew away the smoke. Her hands were shaking. 'I do declare I've ruined my dress,' she croaked. She'd come up behind Zak knowing that like all mad dogs he could not be pacified or stopped and he was liable to do the new girl considerable harm.

'You all saw it,' Dora declared. 'That no-account bum was attempting to murder Betty. Goddamn it, we ain't having no more women killed around here. And I defy anyone to find his belt in Betty's room.'

None of the women made a move to fetch Fox. Jade, however, hot footed it upstairs.

Dora resumed sipping her coffee.

A townsman stuck his head over the batwings, swore violently and ran to fetch the sheriff.

Surprisingly, Jubal had slept soundly. He'd awoken early, washed, put on clean duds and buckled on his gunbelt, whistling as he did so. Jubal wondered whether he had time for breakfast before the storm broke. How long would it be before folk began to wonder why Fox wasn't around? How long before Fox was found locked in his own jailhouse. Jubal had thrown away the keys.

Jubal crossed to the window and stared down at Main Street. He guessed Zak was holed up in one of the saloons. And that suited Jubal just fine. And what the hell was up with that bandy-legged little waddy hot-footing it over to the jailhouse as though he had the devil on his tail.

A small crowd began to gather outside the saloon. And a larger one outside the locked up jailhouse. Sooner or later one of them would figure out that the jailhouse door needed busting open.

As he watched the commotion down on Main Street it began to occur to Jubal that maybe Zak was involved.

FIVE

Jubal eyed Zak's dead body. It was not a pretty sight but Jubal had been a lawman and was used to violent death. The big woman, the one who'd blasted Zak, was now on her second whiskey.

'It wasn't me,' the younger woman Betty, babbled. 'I never stole his money-belt.'

Jubal caught Jade's eye. He reckoned he knew who had separated Zak from his money-belt. However it was not his intention to make Zak's death and the missing money-belt his concern. This time round Jade was lucky. The next occasion might be another matter.

'You ought to have kept a close eye on your pard Marshal Strike,' the saloon-woman Dora advised. Her voice implied he was responsible. Jubal ignored the woman. In any event Zak would have been killed sooner or later. Zak's problem was that he'd been too damn sure of himself.

'Well Zak, I guess I'll just have to manage without your expertise,' Jubal murmured sarcastically.

'Do you think you can!' Dora exclaimed, much to Jubal's surprise. She gulped. 'I've heard tell of the

Cash brothers, Marshal Strike. They are devils, Marshal Strike. Devils!'

Jubal shrugged. To his discomfort he noted both Jade and Dora were staring at him and their expressions plainly told him that they both reckoned he'd not manage at all, not without Zak Bellamy for backup.

Jade rose to her feet. A tall woman, towering over many of the customers, she was an impressive sight. She downed a third whiskey in one gulp.

'What the hell is going on out there? Where's Fox?' Carefully lifting her skirt and petticoats to reveal a trim ankle she stepped over the remains of Zak Bellamy and moved towards the batwings.

Jubal could have told her where Fox was: locked securely in his own jailhouse, but he held his peace.

'Lord they are breaking down the jailhouse door!' Jade announced excitedly.

'You don't say!' Dora joined Jade at the batwings. Betty, still sobbing and shaking, headed slowly upstairs. Jubal sat himself down at the vacated table.

'Give me a beer.' He eyed the smirking bartender Simon.

'Yes sir.' Simon's smirk broadened and the hairs on Jubal's neck bristled.

Jubal sipped the tepid beer. Fox would be some time yet before he arrived. A blacksmith would be needed to get the cell door open.

Flies hovered over and landed on Zak. Zak's own stupidity and inclination to rage had brought about his death, that and Jade's thieving ways.

'There ain't no point in leaving the body lying,' Jubal declared. 'Sheriff Fox won't be of a mind to investigate this matter. You men tote Zak over to

Abilene and then get this mess cleaned up.'

No one argued.

Fox emerged from the cell cussing violently. He'd been made to look a fool. He'd been locked up minus his boots and pants. The pants had been folded and placed on his desk and the boots had been placed beneath his chair. His gunbelt had been hung over the chair and now Fox was left to pull on his pants, stuff his feet into his boots and buckle on his gunbelt under the curious eyes of the townsfolk who now filled his jail.

Folk were demanding loudly what the hell was going on, as if they could not guess and voices demanded the whereabouts of his prisoner. Fools demanded to know what they were going to do about the scheduled hanging. Fox's head felt as though a drum were banging away inside his skull.

'Goddamnit!' Fox yelled furiously, 'I'll ride Strike into the ground. I'll find him. I swear.'

There was a sudden silence until Barnham the barber guffawed loudly.

'Well you ain't got far to ride, Sheriff. Just head on down Main Street until you reach the saloon. You'll find Marshal Strike inside nursing a beer.'

'The hell you say. He ain't left town?'

'Nope,' Barnham responded laconically. Fox had been as drunk as a skunk last night. And this was the result. 'And as for young Zak Bellamy,' Barnham continued gleefully. 'Why just point yourself in the direction of Abilene's funeral parlour and you'll find him sure enough. Not that he got there under his own steam. A couple of the boys toted him over. And I say he got his just deserts. Young Zak tried to strangle one of the girls in plain view of Dora and Jade. We don't want women-killers in our town, Sheriff. What do you say to that!'

'Just get the hell out of my way Barnham.' Fox shoved the barber aside.

'Hold up Sheriff!' Barnham was not done. 'What about O'Banion? You seem to have forgotten him.'

'You damned polecat! Of course I ain't forgotten O'Banion. You men divide yourselves into search parties. Scour this town. Every building. And if anyone objects refer them to me. Any place that varmint could be holed up you look. And when you find him, why hell, that scaffold is ready and waiting.'

Jubal waited. He reckoned it would not be long now. And he was damn right. Fox, face suffused with rage, burst through the batwings and confronted an unperturbed Jubal.

Behind Fox was a sea of faces, all of them alight with anticipation and excitement, there being nothing like the possibility of violent confrontation to brighten up monotonous days.

Calmly Jubal drained the last of his beer. Sure as hell he was outnumbered and outgunned but not, in his opinion, outclassed. Fox was a goddamn fool and no doubt he'd run true to form and prove himself a fool before the eyes of the town.

'Where is he, Strike!' Fox demanded without preamble. 'Speak up, or Lord help me I'll . . .'

'If you mean Zak, why I reckon he's laid out on one of Abilene's tables,' Jubal replied flatly.

Fox levelled the shotgun he was carrying. 'I'm warning you Strike. What the hell have you done with O'Banion?'

'And what makes you think I've done anything with

O'Banion? I'm a lawman like yourself. You told me yourself O'Banion was guilty. This is your town. You ought to know. Your word is good enough for me.'

'You sprung O'Banion!'

Jubal met Fox's accusatory eyes fair and square. 'I don't know what the hell you are talking about.'

'You damn liar, Strike. So help me, I'll pull this trigger.'

'Don't do it. You'll regret it,' Jubal warned.

'The hell I will.' A muscle beneath Fox's eye twitched and Jubal knew with certainty the goddamn lunatic was about to squeeze the trigger.

'You've got it coming,' Fox hollered as he squeezed the trigger half-way through advice from one of others not to do it.

If the shotgun had been loaded Jubal would have been a goner. Jubal had thought beforehand to unload Fox's weaponry and the goddamn fool had not checked the weapons out before hot-footing it in Jubal's direction.

Jubal came to his feet, hefting his own Colt .45 as he did so.

'Goddamn it, Fox, what has gotten into you! What kind of lawman tries to blast a man sitting at a table drinking his beer? Sure as hell you've shown this town what you're made of. Now I'll say this once. Back off. All of you. I ain't going nowhere as yet. Leastways not until I've seen young Zak planted.' Jubal paused. Significantly no one twitched. 'Now I know what it feels like to lose a prisoner,' Jubal continued, 'but I never once felt inclined to gun anyone down in cold blood. And sure as hell I was never fool enough to go gunning for anyone with an unloaded shooter.'

Someone laughed. The laughter dried up abruptly as Fox, his face contorted with fury, swung round cursing.

An older man with a stern and hard-eyed gaze confronted Jubal. 'We'll find O'Banion. And we'll have the truth out of him one way or another before he meets his Maker.'

'And I'll see you hang alongside him, Strike,' Fox spluttered.

Jubal shrugged. 'Well you'd best find O'Banion then, Sheriff.'

'And don't you be forgetting, Sheriff,' a voice broke in, 'that a man is innocent until proved guilty. And in this case only O'Banion can nail his accomplice. We've got to give Marshal Strike the benefit of the doubt.'

'You button your lip, Simon,' Fox snarled. He eyed Jubal contemptuously. 'I'm putting a guard at the livery barn, Strike. You ain't going nowhere. Not without my say-so. Do you hear me?'

Jubal nodded. 'I hear you. And that sounds reasonable to me. Now with your permission, I'll be heading back to the hotel.'

'You do that.' Fox tried to sound as though he were calling the shots although both he and Jubal knew this was not so.

Keeping his eyes peeled for trouble Jubal left the saloon. No one made a move to hinder him. Had Fox reached for his Peacemaker he would have found that weapon also had been unloaded.

Eyes followed Jubal's progress. He could see that the town was already being turned inside out as men searched for O'Banion. Jubal paused beside the scaffold. He eyed the noose meant for O'Banion and

then the nearby table which had been set up. And
the pies were already on the table. Jubal could not.
resist it. Heading towards the table he sent it flying.
Pies scattered and landed in the dirt. And the enter-
prising woman who had set up the table gave an
almighty screech.

Jubal eyed her with disgust. Then he noticed one
of her customers. It was hard not to for the woman
eating the pie was the largest and widest female Jubal
had ever seen. And the ugliest. With a moustache to
boot. A pale, thin, miserable-looking girl stood
beside the huge woman. And then the woman was
moving, heading away down the sidewalk with the
girl trailing behind, leaving Jubal to watch their
progress with idle indifference.

His thoughts turned to Zak. He'd do things right.
He'd wear a suit to the funeral. And have the parson
there to spout a few platitudes.

Fox came out of the saloon. He did not particu-
larly relish the idea of a manhunt. Such ventures,
upon occasion, ended in disaster. And instinct told
him there was no way they'd get O'Banion. He ached
to beat the truth out of Jubal Strike. But Fox
possessed a strong sense of self-preservation. Strike
cornered would be a dangerous beast!

'What the hell are we gonna do, Sheriff?' a
searcher asked despondently. 'There ain't no sign of
the varmint. We've torn this town apart but we ain't
found a sign of him.'

Fox tried to muster enthusiasm. He had to be seen
to be doing right.

'You men who want to ride with me. Let's have
some volunteers. O'Banion is in a bad way. He can't
have got far. Let's see some volunteers.'

Jubal watched sceptically as Fox chose the volunteers to ride along with him. And it was pretty clear to Jubal that the sheriff was picking men who would tire quickly. A worn-out posse would be only too eager to head on back to town proclaiming loudly they'd done their damnedest but without success.

Fox caught Jubal Strike's knowing eye. The bastard was enjoying his discomfort. And Jubal, Fox noted, was not yet on the sidewalk.

Behind Fox the posse mounted up. Fox tried to control his anger. Strike had played him for the fool.

Fox dug in his silver spurs. 'Let's ride!'

With a squeal his horse surged forward. With an oath Jubal jumped aside. The horse missed him but he'd landed awkwardly, twisting his ankle in the process.

'You're slowing down, Strike, slowing down,' Fox hollered and then he was gone.

'Goddamnit!' Jubal heaved himself to his feet. He almost hauled iron, he was so riled. Cussing, he watched the posse dwindle in size until they had become an insignificant speck on the horizon. 'Goddamnit!' he muttered again. Lord there was nothing for it but to hobble back to his hotel room and hole up. He'd need the sawbones no doubt.

'Looks like you won't be heading for Purewater yet a-while Marshal Strike,' a voice announced.

Jubal turned his head. And there was Simon the bartender. Jubal ignored him.

'Come on, Jubal.' Abilene was at Jubal's side. 'I'll help you over to the hotel. Just lean on me.'

'That's mighty generous of you, Abilene.'

'Generosity don't come into it, Jubal. We have a bargain don't we?'

'I reckon.'

The two moved slowly towards the hotel with Jubal leaning heavily on the rotund undertaker.

'Now you blackmailed me into helping out, ain't that a fact?'

'I reckon.'

'But you had sense enough to give your word you would reimburse me handsomely.'

'Yep. Where's this leading? We've had this conversation before!'

'Well I don't reckon you'll be able to raise the sum we agreed. And I ain't of a mind to wait indefinitely.'

'What are you saying?'

'I'm saying I'll give you six months. And if you ain't raised that amount I want a small share of your ranch. A partnership if you like.'

'I'll see you in hell first. I aim to raise the money.'

'Is it a deal?' Abilene persisted.

Jubal halted. Abilene was a lunatic but maybe not a liar.

'I want a solemn vow you'll see O'Banion safely out of this town once he's well enough to ride and the hue and cry has died down.' Jubal paused. 'I ain't lost my memory. I recall what we agreed,' he reassured the undertaker.

'Well I reckon that can be arranged,' Abilene nodded.

'And you'd best bear in mind I may not have a ranch if I don't get this business sorted out. I understand there's a *hombre* by the handle of Jake Day eyeing my spread.'

'You can deal with him, Jubal,' Abilene said, encouragingly.

'Yep. Now I'll shake on the deal. I reckon I can

deal with Day and raise the cash. I don't reckon to be calling you pard.'

Abilene grinned. 'I'll take my chances. You have my word. I'll see O'Banion safely out of town. Yes sir, I can see myself as a ranching man. Now, do you want to see O'Banion?'

'Later maybe. Just get me into the hotel and get the doc.' Jubal paused. 'I trust you. Lord knows why, for you are a lunatic.'

Simon watched Jubal Strike and Abilene. The bartender had spent much of his time observing other folk. It was surprising what could be learnt just from watching, so Simon considered.

He'd bet his boots Strike and Abilene were not strangers. The two had crossed trails previously. Were they friends, Simon wondered. They made an unlikely pair; Abilene was a fat, grinning fool and Strike was a stubborn mule. And, like a mule, none too bright. Why, it was clear as the nose on Simon's face, the fat fool had helped Strike out.

Simon watched and waited. Pretty soon Abilene returned from the hotel and re-entered his funeral parlour. Simon's eyes narrowed speculatively. The funeral parlour, along with the other buildings in town, had been searched, no doubt thoroughly, but it had not been taken apart board by board. Somewhere O'Banion was in there, concealed and sweating, terrified of discovery.

Simon would like nothing better than to denounce Abilene. He'd like to see O'Banion hauled out and frogmarched to the scaffold, and Abilene and Strike along with the horse-thief, but Simon had made contact in a roundabout way with the Cash bothers. And if the two killers were to arrive, expect-

ing to find Strike alive and well, only to discover
Strike had been lynched, well there was no telling
what they'd do. They were capable of turning on an
innocent *hombre*, himself. And they would not be
convinced that Strike's premature death did not
signify. No sir, the reverse would be the case.

Simon pursed his lips. He could still use the knowledge to his advantage. Abilene, running scared,
would pay plenty to save his own miserable hide. And
he'd keep right on paying just as long as was wanted.
Yep, that fat pig would squeal plenty but he would
pay up. Smirking, Simon headed towards the
parlour.

Abilene moved the false panelling. He peered into
the cubbyhole. O'Banion lay still. But alive and well.

'You stay still and quiet,' Abilene ordered. 'Mrs
Webster, my wife, will be fetching over chicken soup
shortly.'

'Thanks,' O'Banion croaked.

'Just thank our mutual friend Jubal. Lord knows
why that stubborn old mule was determined to save
you just as he is determined to hunt down the true
killer.' Abilene grinned. 'And maybe even find Miz
Aggie. Now that proves Jubal is loco. A sane man
would steer clear of that young female. She is nothing but trouble.'

O'Banion grunted. He wasn't sure about Abilene,
not sure at all.

Simon found the door locked. He hammered on it
angrily. He yelled out for Abilene.

'Yes sir,' Abilene was saying, 'Jubal had the notion
to hide you out in a coffin, false bottom and all but
sure as hell I did not reckon that to be humane treat-
ment. This here cubby-hole could have been made

for the task. Normally I just keep a few supplies locked away here but I just knew it was the place for you. Now keep quiet.' The smile vanished from the round, harmless moon-shaped face. 'Not a word, do you hear?' The false wall was replaced, leaving O'Banion helpless for he had not been given a weapon.

'Now what do you want, Simon?'

Simon ignored the smile. He pushed past Abilene and confidently entered the parlour.

Abilene closed the door. He slid the bolt.

'Any man who teams up with Jubal Strike is a fool,' Simon declared. 'And you're a fool, ain't you, Abilene?'

'What do you mean!' Abilene sounded shocked.

'I mean Strike's either bribed you to hide O'Banion or else scared—'

'I don't scare easy.'

'So you say, Abilene. So you say. How would you like to feel the rope around your neck? How would you like to dangle slow, kicking and clawing, and gasping while you strangle real slow with maybe your good wife watching?'

'You're talking nonsense.' Abilene's hand disappeared into his apron-pocket.

'You're an inflated bag of wind, Abilene. And there won't be much left of you by the time this town has finished with you. If I say the word they'll tear this parlour apart, they'll find O'Banion sure enough. What do you say?'

'Why haven't you said the word?' Abilene asked, curious.

'Let's say I don't want to see Jubal torn limb from limb.'

'Why not?'

'That's my business. But I'm willing to risk seeing Jubal torn apart and you along with him if you don't pay up.'

'You can't be trusted. You'd bleed me dry.'

Simon smirked. 'That's a chance you're gonna have to take, lardball.'

'No I ain't.' Abilene kept right on smiling. His hand emerged from his pocket. He placed something in his mouth.

A cigar, Simon thought; the fool aimed to smoke a cigar. The huge belly contracted as Abilene breathed in and then expelled air.

Something struck Simon on the right side of his neck. Instinctively Simon clapped a hand to his neck. And then before he could think to reach for a weapon of his own, he was falling to the floor. And he couldn't move. Not a muscle. But he knew, knew what was happening.

'You're a nobody, Simon,' Abilene declared. 'I ain't having you in my collection. Pride of place can go to the Cash brothers. Yes sir, I reckon you've wired them. You're a villain, Simon, a villain, but you're out of your league. Now look what I've been forced to do to you. I'll get Doc sure enough but he'll be none the wiser. You're gonna die slow Simon, slow and helpless. There ain't no way to combat this poison.' Abilene retrieved the dart. He shook his head. 'You've served your last beer, Simon and that's a fact.' He raised his voice. 'Now don't you be fretting none, O'Banion. I've contracted to see you safe and that's just what I aim to do.'

SIX

The sign proclaimed: ALL ARE WELCOME SAVE SATAN.

Ruben Goodheart surveyed the sign with satisfaction. Beside Ruben stood his son Andrew. The sign had been Andrew's idea.

Not all were pleased. Brother Robert looked decidedly ill at ease.

'Surely not all,' he queried.

'All!' Ruben thundered. 'Without exception all must be given the chance to repent.'

'You haven't thought this through, Pastor. Some must of necessity be turned away. Jubal Strike for one. According to your wife Marshal Strike is heading this way.'

'We have nothing to hide,' Andrew Goodheart smirked.

'The man isn't a fool,' Brother Robert snapped.

'We have nothing to hide,' Ruben Goodheart reiterated. 'Jubal Strike will find nothing to keep him here.'

Brother Robert stood his ground. The Goodhearts were fools or worse. 'Have you ever built a house of cards?' Brother Robert continued. 'Of course you have and you've both seen how that house tumbles.'

'Our house is built on firm ground. My conscience is clear and so should yours be, Brother Robert.' With a snort. Ruben Goodheart turned away.

Jubal Strike, who was heading towards Purewater even as Goodheart was congratulating himself upon the sign, dismounted. Gingerly he tested his ankle. It was bearing up. With a grunt. Jubal wiped the sweat from his brow. There was just no understanding Abilene. The undertaker had been damn keen to get Jubal out of town as quick as possible.

Jubal thought of Simon. Dead and buried and mouldering away. In Abilene Simon had seen a fat genial man of little account, whereas in fact Abilene behind the mask could be as dangerous as a crazed rattlesnake.

Jubal shook his head. Maybe he was damn lucky he had not ended up the same way as Simon. Jubal permitted himself a wry grin, a blow-pipe and poison-dart would not have been something he would have been watching out for. And if his luck failed he would have Abilene as a partner.

Abilene's wife, Miz Coombes – Mrs Webster as she was now – had gotten the idea into her head that Jubal and Abilene could be on their way to becoming cattle barons. Jubal understood that the woman intended dealing with the paperwork. She'd keep the accounts and every dollar would count, accord-ing to Abilene.

'Hell on earth,' Jubal groaned. 'Hell on earth.' What had possessed him to save O'Banion's hide? And saved it was. Abilene would sneak O'Banion out of town when it was safe to do so.

'Like yourself,' Abilene had declared, 'I'm a man of my word.' He'd grinned. '*Partner,*' he'd added for good measure. 'You won't regret it,' he'd continued. 'Honest toil is all we know but Mrs Webster has a mind to invest in our venture and . . .'

'You're right,' Jubal had declared. 'I'd best be getting to Purewater.' It occurred to him that only a woman not right in the head could have lived with Abilene all these years.

Resting a while, Jubal rolled himself a smoke. In Jubal's opinion Purewater stank. Bones were beginning to appear on the tortuous twisted route which led to Purewater. Bones of yolk who had clearly perished on the trail. Oddly there were only human bones which indicated that these unfortunate pilgrims had been on foot. Jubal had also surmised they'd been without footwear and weapons of any kind. There'd been no discarded canteens either, so they'd been travelling without water. The poor devils would have indeed considered the harsh landscape to be Satan's country as they perished beneath the remorseless heat of the sun.

Bluntly, these folk had been turned adrift to die.

Clearly Ruben Goodheart had been responsible for the turning. And quite likely these folk were the unfortunate sheep who had wanted to quit Ruben's flock.

By riding into Purewater Jubal felt as though he were putting his head on the block. But it had to be done. His conviction had grown. A crazed killer of women was holed up in Purewater. Jubal aimed to root the villain out.

And there was Aggie of course. The cause of

Jubal's present predicament. Jubal cursed Aggie. And then felt ashamed, for she might have fallen victim to the as yet unnamed killer.

Resolutely Jubal continued on his way. One way or another he'd get the truth out of Ruben Goodheart.

Ruben Goodheart was uneasy. A marshal turning up in Purewater was something he had not foreseen. To his annoyance he found himself questioning his stupid wife as to what little she might have heard about Strike. And from what she said it was not long before Ruben had formed the opinion that trouble travelled in Strike's wake.

Two deaths and a jail-break spoke for themselves. True, the death of the man Zak Bellamy and the fate of the bartender Simon could not be attributed to Strike but the disappearance of the condemned man was too much of a coincidence. Clearly Strike was a meddler. And now because of Mrs Goodheart's love of gossip the community of Purewater was aware that Jubal Strike was heading their way. No question, the knowledge would unsettle the doubters amongst the community.

Ruben reached a decision. It would be for the good of all if Jubal Strike were to have a change of direction. Strike must be kept away from Purewater. Ruben's right eye twitched, a sure sign that he was disturbed.

Across the table Mrs Goodheart regarded her husband. Her jaws chomped. Eating was one way of getting back at Ruben. He could rant about gluttony all he wished but it would be of no avail.

Last night Jubal had eaten something which had disagreed with him mightily. He reckoned that it must have been the cheese. And he was forced to admit that, like that lump of mouldering cheese, he had seen better days. He'd actually dreamt of the Cash brothers and a disturbing dream it had been.

He had dreamt those two roughnecks had gotten the better of him, that they aimed to honour their pledge to roast him. He had awoken kicking and thrashing, convinced he'd been fixed to the spit and placed over the fire and that the flames were reaching out for him.

Dusk was falling now and it was time to make camp. Jubal found himself glancing around warily, which was loco. The Cash brothers were not hereabouts. Not yet. Nevertheless he knew he could not bed down beside the fire and take his chances.

He must of necessity hole up amongst the rocks, forgoing his bedroll and blankets which must be left close to the camp-fire whilst he bedded down, cold and uncomfortable. He cursed the Cash brothers and those who had freed them.

Not one voice in the community of Purewater commented when Ruben rode out. He had done so before, his reason being, as he gave out, that he needed to be alone in the wilderness.

Mrs Goodheart was glad to see him go, although she made a show of pretending otherwise. Others were glad as well, especially those folk who believed Marshal Strike might be of help.

Ruben could hardly bear to bid his son Andrew a goodbye. Andrew had been loudly proclaiming that he himself would help Marshal Strike fit into the community. Ruben found himself agreeing with Brother Robert's opinion that Andrew must be loco. No man in his right mind would want to see Strike part of the community, although, for the sake of appearances, one might have to pretend. Andrew however had been overly enthusiastic. All Andrew wanted to do was challenge his pa.

A short distance from the settlement Ruben found the marker. It had been newly placed, for it had not been there previously. The sight of it sent the blood rushing to his head and his heart pounding, for one of his people was responsible.

Someone had dared to set up a sign which proclaimed in red paint the words DEAD MAN'S TRAIL. Sweating, he removed the marker and cast it into the brush. Next time the community gathered he would have them all pray for forgiveness. The guilty one would know what it was all about.

Ruben rode on. He planned to confront Jubal Strike on the trail. He planned to lull Strike into a sense of security, then blast him out of the saddle. As it turned out, Ruben encountered Strike's camp-fire, the embers of which, like a beacon in the darkness, called out to Ruben.

Jubal had drifted into an uneasy sleep. As he dreamed the leering faces of Sid and Tom Cash had floated before him in the darkness. And this time around he could not blame the cheese. The faces had become wolflike, rushing towards him, mouths open. His eyes had jerked open and he'd been awake again, cold and uncomfortable and trying to get some shut-eye.

Just as he had almost sunk into deep sleep the sound of shale crunching beneath a boot awoke him. His eyes jerked open but it took a mite longer for his head to grasp the fact that booted feet were approaching his camp.

Slowly his hand moved towards the butt of his .45. The handle was cool and reassuring to his hand. Carefully he withdrew the weapon and waited.

Lord his back felt stiff. It was a wonder it did not creak. His eyes probed the darkness and pretty soon he was able to make out the dark shape of a man cautiously approaching the camp.

Ruben focused upon the shape of Strike bedded down beside the still-glowing embers of the camp-fire. The sleeping man must be Strike. It could be no other.

Ruben tried to still his breathing. It sounded harsh to his ears. He sighted his rifle. He was close and could not miss at this range. The sleeping man did not move.

For an instant Ruben hesitated as thoughts flooded into his mind, thoughts about how wrong it had all gone. He could not exactly pin-point the moment the rottenness had set in. His dream had turned sour. Instinct told him that unless he got rid of Strike pronto his dream would be over.

The matter resolved Ruben, at point blank range, fired three shots in rapid succession. He then retreated unwillingly to view his handiwork.

Jubal could have killed the bushwhacker. But he stayed his hand. The attacker could only be Ruben Goodheart. Goodheart had gotten wind of his approach and had decided to act rather than wait upon his arrival.

Jubal smiled grimly. Sure as hell Goodheart must have plenty to hide. And Goodheart's face when he discovered he had loused up would be worth seeing. Jubal was looking forward to it.

During the time he'd spent resting up his ankle Jubal had learnt something of Goodheart's set-up. Goodheart's community was not as entirely isolated as Goodheart would have liked it to be. Like everyone else his people had to eat. Supplies had to be taken up to the settlement and these supplies were taken up by mule train.

Goodheart's henchmen – from time to time – descended on Osborne to buy their provisions. But none of the murders, according to Abilene, had occurred whilst these elders, as they called themselves, had been around town.

Goodheart's people also traded in horses. According to Abilene, Goodheart had a lucrative contract to supply Fort William with horse flesh.

Abilene had also informed Jubal that none of the victims had seemingly put up a struggle. They'd all been taken by surprise.

Jubal and Fox had again exchanged harsh words. Fox, having had the town scoured once again, had given up on O'Banion proclaiming that as he wasn't in town he must either be long gone or dead. He'd done his darnedest and there was nothing else to be done. He'd also loudly expressed the opinion that it was damn lucky for Jubal Strike that O'Banion had not been found because one way or another the truth would out.

Fox had also told Jubal to get the hell out of his town as soon as Jubal could walk. 'Too bad I missed you,' he'd also snarled.

Jubal had rejoined that he ought to have blasted Fox.

Fox had replied by accusing Jubal of dishonouring his badge.

The two had parted company, each condemning the other.

Bedding down once again Jubal put Fox out of his mind, although being accused of dishonouring his badge sure as hell rankled.

The following morning, when Jubal approached Purewater, at a leisurely pace, he saw that Goodheart's settlement would not be taken unawares. They'd had the foresight to set look-outs, which in these violent times was a prudent move. Flashing mirrors had alerted Jubal to the presence of the watchers.

Riding forward Jubal felt a tightness between his shoulder blades. He was a sitting duck and he knew it. But shots did not materialize. Ruben Goodheart, if he were about was seemingly not one to murder openly. Maybe Goodheart was one of these *hombres* who put great store in keeping up appearances. Jubal had met that kind before.

The settlement of Purewater was situated in a safe enough place. To get into it, one had to enter a canyon whose entrance was clearly guarded.

Jubal squinted in disbelief. A large sign had been set up at the entrance to the canyon, a sign painted in red, which proclaimed that all were welcome save Satan.

That sign, had Goodheart but realized it, was enough to make any sane *hombre* execute a smart about-turn. Only a desperate man or a fool would want to ride on into Purewater after seeing such a sign.

Jubal reckoned he himself was both: a desperate man and a fool. Right now he ought to be at his ranch and here he was riding into this loco set-up.

Two black-garbed *hombres*, each casually toting a rifle, stepped out to greet him.

'Welcome, brother. Would you care to dismount?'

Jubal did not care but as he was not being given a choice he slowly swung down from the saddle. The two *hombres* introduced themselves as Brother Saul and Brother David.

'So what brings you to Purewater, Marshal Strike?' Brother Saul asked with an ingratiating smile.

'I was expected then!' Jubal observed. Seemingly Goodheart had not chosen to spread the word that Jubal Strike would not be arriving.

Brother Saul nodded. 'What brings you to Purewater Marshal?'

Jubal thinned his lips. 'I need to speak with Pastor Goodheart. You could say I'm in need of help.'

'Then you've come to the right man, Brother Strike.' Brother Saul paused, then smiled again. 'All are welcome, Brother Strike, but weapons of death are not. You must leave your weapons.'

Jubal felt inclined to point out that Saul and David were not following their own rules but that would have been a waste of breath. Without a word he carefully unbuckled his gunbelt and handed it over. His rifle followed.

'And the knife!' Brother David ordered.

Jubal withdrew his knife from his boot.

'And now if you don't mind, Brother Strike, we will check you and your belongings over just in case you've overlooked anything.'

Jubal shrugged. He did not argue. And that, he saw, surprised the brothers.

Without opposition, Jubal rode into Purewater. The disturbing thought occurred to him that once anyone got into Ruben's town they would find it damn hard to leave.

*

Pretty soon Jubal was able to observe that what was good for some was not good for all. Certain *hombres* in Purewater toted rifles. Jubal reckoned they must be Goodheart's trusted henchmen. It made sense. A town could not leave itself at the mercy of whoever might ride in.

Images of Sid and Tom Cash invaded Jubal's mind. Those two would sure make themselves at home in a settlement where few toted a weapon.

As Jubal rode into the settlement no one challenged him. Indeed no one paid him much attention at all. Folk just went about their business without sparing him even a glance. And yet he knew they were aware of his presence amongst them.

He dismounted before what would have passed for a livery barn, in a normal town that is.

'How much?'

The gaunt-looking *hombre* merely grinned. 'This is Purewater, brother. There is no charge. There's also no saloon nor is there a bath-house. Water is in short supply hereabouts. There's a boarding-house,' the ostler continued, 'set up especially for strangers.'

'Anything else I ought to know?' Jubal essayed.

The ostler nodded. 'Yep. You have two choices, Marshal Strike. Move out or join us. The choice is yours. It is not a decision to be taken lightly so you'll be given time enough to ponder.'

'And if I don't join you?'

'Well, you must move on. You can't stay around.' The man grinned. 'You'd be an unsettling influence.'

'Take good care of my horse.'

'That's what I'm here for.'

'Where do I find Goodheart?'

'Try the meeting-house Marshal Strike. It's the big place, painted white, so you can't miss it.'

Jubal headed for the meeting-house. Folk still would not meet his eye. But he sensed his every move was being noted. Arriving at the meeting-house Jubal drew back his foot and then brought the heel of his boot forward and hard against the meeting-house door. The kick failed to make an impression on the door itself but the noise was loud enough to awaken Goodheart should he be snoozing inside.

The door flew open with a vengeance and a furious countenance confronted Jubal.

'Don't you know . . .' the words dried away as Ruben Goodheart saw who had disturbed his solitude. Goodheart's mouth dropped open.

Jubal smiled crookedly. 'Howdy Pastor Goodheart. I reckon it's time we had a palaver about a certain matter.'

Ruben Goodheart was a man of middling years whose grey hair was worn cropped close to the skull. A closely clipped moustache adorned a narrow upper lip. Goodheart's skin was lined and bags hung beneath green, almost reptilian, eyes.

Goodheart's face blanched. 'Strike,' he croaked, unable to hide his disbelief.

'That's me right enough.' Jubal stepped inside. He kicked the meeting-house door shut behind him. 'You look surprised to see me, Pastor Goodheart. Why is that, I wonder?'

'This is a peaceful place. We have no need of lawmen,' Goodheart croaked.

'Well that answer just won't do. I reckon this settlement had word of my coming. You're the only *hombre* looking surprised around here, Ruben. Maybe you thought me dead!'

Ruben Goodheart pulled himself together. This was his town. He was in charge.

'So Marshal Strike what brings you to Purewater?' he demanded, drawing himself up to his full height. He was taller, he noted, than Jubal Strike.

Jubal's gaze had dropped to Goodheart's hands. The man possessed long bony fingers. Coarse black hair sprouted from the backs of these fingers. Jubal imagined those fingers dripping with blood as Goodheart butchered an unfortunate female who'd just been rendered insensible.

Lifting his eyes he met Goodheart's gaze. 'It says all are welcome.'

'Quite so.' Goodheart folded his arms. 'Now I'll ask you again, Marshal Strike. What is it you want? How can I help you?'

Jubal had not worked out a plan. He eyed Goodheart before formulating a response.

'I'm a plain-speaking man, Pastor Goodheart. I'm here because I aim to find out what has become of Miz Agatha Keeley. She's wanted back home and I am charged with finding her.'

'I know no one of that name. You've had a wasted journey.'

'If you want to see me ride out you had best tell me what I want to know. Now I could be asking you about the bones scattered along the trail, but what I am asking you concerns Aggie. Now I know you know the girl. You knew a Dan Keeley once. Weren't you boyhood friends?'

'Hardly that, Marshal Strike.'

'You knew Dan Keeley,' Jubal reiterated, obstinately.

'Not well.' Goodheart hesitated. 'Daniel Keeley saved my life. Many years ago.'

'You met his family.'

'I may have done,' Goodheart hedged.

'Sure as hell you did,' Jubal declared. 'And that young vixen Aggie has a mighty good memory. She'd remember you right enough, Pastor Goodheart. She recognized you on Harlots' Row.'

'That's a lie.' Goodheart raised his hands. His fists were clenched and the knuckles gleamed white. Pastor Goodheart looked more than ready to launch himself at Jubal Strike.

'No it ain't,' Jubal replied, forcing himself to evince a calmness he did not feel. 'What did you do? Kill her?'

'I did not touch a hair of her head. I swear!'

'Well I'm not talking about her head. What about her neck? Maybe you grabbed and squeezed and throttled the breath out of her.'

'You're insane, Strike.' Goodheart was breathing hard. His hand closed over a heavy brass candlestick.

Jubal tensed. Any moment now Goodheart would lash out with the candlestick.

'Just tell me what happened, Goodheart. When I've got what I want, I'll go.' And sure as hell Goodheart wanted him gone.

Goodheart took the bait. 'I may have scared her,' he admitted.

'May?' Jubal pressed.

'No decent woman dresses as a man and parades up and down such a place.'

'And you told her so.'

'I may have done.'

Jubal nodded. 'It would take more than a bawling-out to unsettle Miz Aggie. What aren't you telling me?'

'She may have misread my intention.'

'How so?' Jubal asked, his voice dangerously low.

Goodheat coughed. 'She may have thought I intended taking hold of her by the shoulders. That's all. She moved quickly. She ran off.'

'You lost your temper and made a grab for her intending, let's say, to shake the life out of her. Figuratively speaking, let's say Aggie dodged you, was scared out of her wits and scarpered.' Jubal kept his last thought to himself. Maybe, just maybe Goodheart had been ready to explode with rage because Aggie had demanded money to keep the knowledge of his activities to herself. 'What else,' Jubal concluded, 'what else ought I to know?'

Goodheart replaced the candlestick. 'There isn't much to tell, Marshal Strike. The following day I searched for Agatha. She was gone, disappeared without a trace.' He shook his head. 'And no wonder the sheriff was also hunting for that young woman. An item of jewellery was missing, I believe. It was presumed she had stolen it.' Goodheart paused, 'For what it's worth, Marshal Strike, I believe that resourceful young woman,' sarcasm laced Goodheart's voice, 'concealed herself upon a wagon train heading for Red Bute Pass.'

'Red Bute Pass. Why the hell wasn't I told!'

'Well it was hardly a train, Marshal Strike. Just three wagons, farming folk headed for Red Bute. And I am sure Sheriff Flock would not have realized—'

'All right,' Jubal broke in. 'Knowing Aggie that sounds plausible.'

'Then you'll head for Red Bute Pass and verify my assumption?'

Jubal was tempted.

'I'm not going anywhere, Marshal Strike. My place is here. If you fail to find that Agatha Keeley ever was in Red Bute Pass you can return.'

'And don't think I won't. If you have lied, if you have harmed Aggie, you're going to know hell on earth,' Jubal vowed.

'Then I have nothing to fear from you, Marshal Strike.'

'Aggie's got to wait.' Jubal met Goodheart's startled gaze. 'You'll know about the killer who has been stalking and killing womenfolk in Fox's town. You'll know that Fox is damn useless when it comes to law-keeping. And you'll also know that the killer is right here in Purewater. I aim to root him out. I'm a lawman, Goodheart. I can't walk away.' Jubal paused. 'So now what do you have to say?'

SEVEN

Goodheart snorted dismissively.

'You're mad, Strike, completely loco. Your killer isn't here.' Goodheart paused. 'You're a trouble-maker by nature,' he declared, 'and we have ways of dealing with your kind.'

'I reckon you do,' Jubal rejoined drily. He shrugged. 'First thing I aim to do, with your agree-ment naturally, is check out this place. If Aggie's been here, I'll know it.'

'You're obsessed with that woman. Obsessed,' Goodheart ground out.

'And then I aim to check into the guest-house.'

'I'd advise you to leave after you've concluded your fruitless search,' Goodheart rejoined, his voice unnaturally quiet.

Jubal grinned. He was getting to Goodheart. 'I'm taking your sign at face value. "All" it says. "Save Satan". Well, I certainly ain't Satan. Even you can't convince those deluded fools I'm Satan come amongst 'em.'

'I wouldn't bet on that, Strike. This settlement is for the righteous. Not for saddlebums such as your-self. Those who do not join us have to leave. It is one

91

of our rules. If you don't go willingly, you'll be driven out.'

Jubal regarded Goodheart speculatively. 'I reckoned that whilst I was here the killer would make a move to dispose of me.' He thinned his lips. 'That move has been made. Should I draw my own conclusions?'

Goodheart opened his mouth as if to deny the accusation. But then his lips clamped together and he contented himself with hard-eyeing Jubal.

Jubal spat. 'You can't bring yourself to admit to being a low-down lousy bushwhacker, can you? Well I reckon we understand one another, Pastor Goodheart.'

'I believe we do.'

Jubal hooked his thumbs into his belt. He felt vulnerable without the reassuring weight of his Colt .45. He continued to eye Goodheart and then decided that he might as well speak plainly. Goodheart already knew that he'd cottoned on to what was happening in Purewater.

'And once anyone joins up it's for life, ain't it, Pastor Goodheart?' Jubal continued mockingly. 'No one ever leaves. And them that try to why they fall by the wayside. And that ain't surprising. Folk afoot without water nor boots nor victuals, why, they don't fare well, do they!'

Goodheart folded his arms. He met Jubal's gaze squarely.

'We are a community of over fifty decent, hardworking souls. And you, Strike, are just one man making wild and unsubstantiated accusations. You belong in an asylum, Strike. Now get out of my sight. Search for that female if you must.'

Jubal shrugged, 'I'll see you around, Goodheart. You can count upon it.'

Big Jade, the saloon-woman, was a thief and a liar. But she had never been a fool. She was as cunning and smart as they came. Indeed, she considered herself a damn sight smarter than any man.

When Jubal Strike confronted Pastor Ruben Goodheart, Jade was lounging against the bar. Through carefully lowered lids she studied Abilene. Now Jade had always figured Simon to be a healthy enough *hombre* and she found it mighty strange that Simon had been taken with a mysterious seizure right there in Abilene's parlour.

Abilene's expression was always jovial. But he was a man who said little. And he had never had any dealings with any of the girls. When approached he would grin and say Mrs Webster was woman enough for any man.

Jade found herself reflecting uneasily that maybe Abilene was the woman-killer who'd been preying on the town's women. And maybe Simon had figured it out. And paid for being too smart.

Jade downed her whiskey. She had one almighty pain in the guts and she'd had enough of the saloon and its men. Uncharacteristically she decided she would quit early tonight. She'd go on home and brew up tea and have an early night.

Impassively Abilene watched the big woman throw a shawl over her shoulders and march out, face like thunder. Things were going well. O'Banion was gone now. Abilene had seen him safely out of town when the hue and cry had died down.

'Lord, I hope Jubal knows what kind of pard he'll

be getting if he can't raise the cash,' O'Banion had observed as he'd ridden away.

Abilene sighed. His wife had gotten it into her head that himself and Jubal were destined to be cattle barons. The Cash brothers would have to be taken care of. With Jubal dead there'd be no partnership.

Outside dusk was falling and it was beginning to rain. Jade, anxious to be home, quickened her pace.

She was passing an alleyway when she heard a low moan and a cry for help.

'What the hell!' Jade peered into the alleyway. She would never have gone in if she had not seen the shape of a woman huddled at the back of the alleyway.

Jade entered the alleyway. 'What's amiss?' The other woman was big but Jade was bigger.

As Jade headed into the alleyway a sixth sense warned her that something was not quite right. Her hand crept into her pocket and closed over the handle of her blade. Most of the girls were damn fools but not she. She was always prepared for the worst.

'Help me,' the shape groaned.

Helping folk was not Jade's forte but maybe she was getting soft.

Abilene sipped his beer. Yes sir, Mrs Webster was busily designing a brand for the partnership and . . .

The batwings burst open and big Jade staggered into the saloon. Blood stained her gown and was smeared over her face and hands. One dangling hand, Abilene observed, held a bloodstained blade.

Silence descended.

'It's Bill Deeds,' Jade croaked. 'He's the goddamn

killer. That there horse-thief was innocent.' She collapsed on to a chair. 'The brute dresses up as a woman and lures helpless females into the alleyway and then he chloroforms 'em and . . .' Jade seized a whiskey bottle. Raising it to her lips she drank deeply.

'Well I reckon Bill Deeds will be needing my services,' Abilene observed. The whole town knew good old Bill Deeds the farrier. Abilene squinted at Jade. Hell, if that woman wanted to change professions she must have the strength required to do Bill's job. Bill had been sturdy enough but Jade must have the strength of an ox.

A sobering thought hit Abiilene.

Goddamnit! Strike had jumped to the wrong conclusion. Now if this Miz Aggie were not in Purewater, Strike had no business delaying. Whilst Strike was time-wastling anything at all could be happening to their joint venture, the ranch.

Abilene brought his glass down upon the table with violence. The glass shattered. There was only one thing for it. Of necessity he must himself ride to Purewater and collect Strike.

'Goddamn Miz Aggie!' Abilene exclaimed. 'She's at the root of this trouble.'

No one was listening. The saloon was emptying fast as men poured out, anxious to take a look at Bill Deeds.

'And the sonofabitch made out he liked me,' Jade was saying.

'Too bad,' Abilene muttered. Too bad he must reserve his last two jars for the Cash brothers, Bill might have made an interesting addition to the collection.

Jade downed what was left in the whiskey bottle. 'Ain't it,' she muttered in agreement.

Jubal had to take his hat off to Goodheart. The man's stamina was surely amazing. Goodheart could rant and rave for hours without flagging.

There was no chance of nodding off whilst Goodheart raved and indeed the congregation listened intently with a kind of glazed expression on their faces. Some chose to wander around the meeting-hall, hands raised high, swaying from side to side, so affected were they by Goodheart's words.

Jubal, to his displeasure, had discovered that there were no time limits to these get-togethers. Goodheart kept right on going for as long as the mood took him. Hours. And the singing and chanting were something to behold. Folk bawled themselves hoarse.

Jubal, who'd been bench sitting for almost three hours, found he could stomach no more of Goodheart. He wiped his brow, rose to his feet and, trying not to step on any toes, made his escape.

Baccy was not allowed in Purewater. And now Jubal, as he stood outside the meeting-house found he needed baccy mighty bad. How anyone could stomach life in Purewater he did not comprehend.

'Marshal Strike, Marshal Strike, a word if you please,' a voice called.

Jubal squinted in the direction of the voice. She would have a word if he pleased or not. Nor was she the first to be wanting a word.

Jubal headed for the alleyway where Jane Goodheart lurked.

'I want you to take me with you when you leave,'

she told him without preamble.

'Well I ain't ready to leave yet a while Miss Jane,' Jubal replied. 'There's a murdering bushwhacker on the loose and he may be here.'

'Definitely not, Marshal Strike,' Jane Goodheart rejoined briskly.

'And how do you know that, ma'am?' Jubal essayed.

'Well it's obvious Marshal Strike,' Jane Goodheart replied without hesitation. 'You must see it.'

'How so?'

'Father does not care for solitude. He maintains solitude affords a sinner a chance to doubt and commit wrongdoing. You never see anyone walking around here alone do you, Marshal Strike? We travel in pairs. Father is the sole exception. No man from here would have been able to roam Osborne alone. Or even ride out of here alone.'

Jubal digested the information. It was true. Folk did not walk solo. There were always two of them together. Folk worked in pairs hereabouts. He'd never paid any heed to this until now.

'Why didn't you make a break for it in Osborne?' Jubal asked curiously. 'You go there with your ma from time to time.'

'I was afraid, Marshal Strike. I've been told that if I cause trouble I'll be locked in the cellar and never see the light of day.'

Jubal nodded. 'That sounds like your pa. Fear and fervour, that's one way of keeping folk in line.'

'Will you help me leave Marshal Strike?' she asked. 'Miss Agatha Keeley is not here and has never been here.'

Jubal nodded. 'I reckon,' he agreed. 'But I can't

turn a blind eye to what has been going on here, Miss Jane. It cannot be allowed to continue. Your pa and the elders have been making damn sure that any quitters meet a grisly fate. Maybe you know that.'

'I suspected something, Marshal Strike. But I am uncertain . . .'

'I'll spell it out for you, ma'am. Your pa and the elders go after any folk that ride out. They let 'em get so far, then relieve them of their horses, and water, and victuals and boots. The quitters are just turned adrift, Miss Jane. There ain't one that's made it safe to Osborne. Bones litter the trail. But then you must have seen them.'

Miss Jane hung her head, 'I didn't want to believe,' she murmured. 'And not everyone will know. Only mother and myself are allowed into Osborne. The other women and children stay here.'

'You get along home now,' Jubal advised. 'Things ain't going on like they have been doing, Miss Jane. You have my word.' He did not inform her that he had said the same to half a dozen other folk eager to quit Purewater.

'Thank you.' She slipped away glancing fearfully around as she did so.

Jubal knew Goodheart wanted him dead. But murder could not be done openly. Appearances must be maintained. Goodheart would know that Jubal had worked out what had been happening here. Goodheart was biding his time. Jubal had an uneasy feeling Goodheart intended to strike and strike pretty soon.

'Goddamnit!' Jubal exclaimed in disbelief. A *hombre* was riding into Purewater. The last *hombre* Jubal had expected to see.

'Lord Strike, I have had a hell of a time finding this goddamn place!' Abilene exclaimed as he dismounted, slapping dust from his clothes as he did so. 'I ain't accustomed to horse travel. Nor do I care for it.'

'Have you news of Aggie?' Jubal tried to hide his eagerness.

'Goddamnit, Strike, can't you think of anything other than Miz Aggie!'

'Then why are you here? Is it the ranch?'

Abilene shook his head. 'I'm here to tell you that you've been following the wrong trail, Strike. That goddamn murdering varmint ain't holed up in Purewater. He was in Osborne all along. Right under our noses. It was good old Bill Deeds who was the killer.' Abilene cackled. 'The damn fool made the mistake of tangling with big Jade. Naturally Deeds came off worse. He's planted now and planted deep.'

'Head intact, I trust,' Jubal observed drily. He was prepared to take Abilene's say-so that Deeds was the killer.

'Yep. Last time I looked his head was on his neck.' Abilene smiled crookedly. 'I'm saving my last two jars for the Cash brothers. Yes sir, I reckon they'll show up in Osborne.' He paused. 'What's your news, Jubal?'

'Well Miss Aggie may be at Red Bute Pass,' Jubal answered.

'So we'll head to Red Bute tomorrow. It's time this matter was settled. You have a ranch to run, Jubal Strike. And I still reckon to be your partner.'

'Well it ain't possible to leave yet,' Jubal rejoined. 'You don't know it all, Abilene. I've business with Ruben Goodheart and the elders. They are wrongdoers, Abilene. You've seen the bones on the trail. Well that is their work. Folk have been turned adrift on foot without water or victuals. And there are folk who want to leave here. They're counting on me to get them out.'

Abilene shook his head. 'Leave matters be, Jubal. These folk ain't your concern. No one made them join Goodheart. These pilgrims came of their own volition.'

'We're talking cold-hearted murder here,' Jubal argued. 'Turning folk adrift is murder.'

Abilene snorted. He seemed not to care. 'Well you have a dilemma then, Jubal.' He shook his head. 'What do you think of big Jade? She sure is one crazy female. And Bill Deeds dressing himself up as a woman to lure unsuspecting females into alleyways! I ain't told you that part, have I, Jubal? That was how he managed to catch them unawares. But not Jade.'

Jubal shrugged. The less said about big Jade the better. The woman was a thief and she had killed Zak. Maybe if Zak had been longer in the tooth he would have realized women and whiskey did not mix. A man needed a clear head when dealing with women, especially a woman such as big Jade.

'I can see you ain't in a talkative mood, Strike,' Abilene observed. 'Just show me a bed will you? And then let me sleep. I'll be a goner as soon as my head touches the pillow.'

'Well you'd best make the acquaintance of Goodheart and his elders first,' Jubal replied. 'And you'll have to check in the hardware. They'll search you as well for any hidden blades or baccy.'

'Baccy!' Abilene exclaimed in disbelief.

'Yep. Baccy. Goodheart may feel obliged to countenance murder. Just to keep folk from quitting his flock, mind you. But sure as hell he don't feel obliged to countenance baccy. It's been banned in Purewater.'

The Purewater guest-house was not much of a place. It saw few guests. The mattresses were worn and the rooms sparsely furnished. Jubal left Abilene sleeping. He returned to his own room and stretching out on the bed thought of Bill Deeds.

He recalled his last sighting of the brawny blacksmith. Deeds had been stripped to the waist. He had been shoeing Jubal's horse at the time.

Jubal reflected sourly that had Deeds been wearing a shirt he would have been laughing up his sleeve at Marshal Jubal Strike.

'Good luck, Marshal Strike,' Deeds had said, adding, 'If anyone can winkle out this killer it will be you. I never believed it was O'Banion.'

Deeds should have let things be and yet his unnatural urges had driven him out once again to kill. Jubal shook his head. Deeds would have gotten away with it if he had let things be.

Goodheart possessed a different kind of madness. Goodheart could not let things be. He could not let those who wanted to go simply leave the community. Fear tied these people to Goodheart just as much as fervour. Together fear and fervour added up to a powerful combination.

Lying on his bed Jubal considered various possibilities. The linchpins here were Goodheart and his elders. It was they who were resolved to keep this crazy set-up going at whatever the cost. And the cost was high. The cost was snuffed-out lives.

Jubal said as much to Abilene some time later

when Abilene's head emerged from underneath the coarse grey blanket. Abilene was one of those folk who awaken instantly. He heard Jubal out in silence.

'So you're determined to take them on!'

Jubal nodded. 'There ain't no other way. But first I aim to get my weaponry back. Goodheart keeps the weapons secured in a room back of the meeting-hall.'

'What about our deal?' Abilene asked unexpectedly.

Jubal snorted with exasperation. 'It still stands if that's what you're asking. If I don't pay you what I agreed to pay for your help with O'Banion within the set time you come in as a pardner.' He grinned. 'But don't raise your hopes. I'm damn sure you're gonna be paid. And I ain't aiming to get planted here in Purewater. I've dealt with the likes of Goodheart before. My luck will hold good.'

Abilene passed no comment, merely nodded before enquiring, 'So who are the folk wanting to quit this crazy place?'

Jubal shrugged. 'I don't aim to name names. But. let's say I believed Jane Goodheart when she told me her pa is capable of locking her in the cellar and not letting her see light of day again should she put a foot wrong.'

Abilene whistled. 'So when are you planning on going after your weaponry, Jubal?'

'It's got to be soon,' Jubal replied. 'I reckon it'll have to be this coming Sunday. After the last sermon of the day Goodheart and the elders hole up at Goodheart's place for a celebratory supper. Ma Goodheart and Jane wait on them hand and foot.'

Abilene nodded again. 'You won't be the only

hombre who has tried to get his weaponry back. Have you thought of that?'

Jubal met Abilene's gaze squarely. 'I have.' He paused. 'I take it you ain't interested in helping out the folk who want to leave.'

'You take it right. I ain't putting my neck in a noose for a bunch of crazy loons. If they weren't crazy they wouldn't be here.'

'Well there ain't no reason for you to stay around. You've delivered the news concerning Deeds. You head back to Osborne. Do it now.'

'That's what I aim to do. But I'll choose my own time to leave. I'm my own man, Jubal Strike, and always will be.'

'There will be a mule train coming in tomorrow,' Jubal observed. 'They'll deliver the goods and then head out. I suggest you ride with them. This settlement is a powder-keg just waiting to go up.'

'I said I'm my own man,' Abilene reiterated.

Jubal shrugged. 'If you get caught in the crossfire then it's on your own fool head.'

'I've got a better head than you, Strike, as you'll discover. Now, if you'll excuse me, I aim to mosey around and become better acquainted with Goodheart's people.'

Leaving Strike, Abilene set about wandering around Goodheart's community. The people he found were suspicious and hostile but Abilene, playing the part of an affable none-too-bright undertaker began to win a few over.

Although no one would say so openly they were all mighty interested in the Osborne murders and the murderer himself, the blacksmith Bill Deeds.

Abilene chatted with anyone who gave him the

time of day making it clear that now his message had been delivered to Strike he would be returning to Osborne pretty damn quick.

Goodheart's only reaction was a curt nod. It was hard to know what Goodheart might be thinking but then Abilene had never given a damn about such matters. His mind was occupied with various possibilities. He knew better than to share these possibilities with Jubal Strike.

For an isolated community such as Purewater the arrival of a mule train was a big event although Goodheart might like to pretend this was just a normal day.

From first light an air of expectancy pervaded the little community. Otherwise dismal gloomy faces were observed to smile. And Goodheart was wise enough to relax his rules and allow the men of the community to pass the time of day with the drovers. Womenfolk were a separate matter and as always they were kept in their place, expected to hang back and watch the new arrivals from afar.

Jubal also watched. Letters had been brought, he saw, and these were eagerly snatched up. And letters which had been written, all Jubal suspected, scrutinized by the elders, were handed over. Goods were unloaded and toted to the storehouse. And all the while the elders hung around keeping a watchful eye on everybody.

Abilene, Jubal noted, was not about. Abilene, Jubal decided, was as stubborn as an old mule and if he wasn't yet ready to leave there would be nothing Jubal could do to change Abilene's mind.

Jubal Strike, Abilene reflected, was a darn fool, and certainly needed saving from himself. Guile was a weapon Jubal had as yet not learned to appreciate.

Upon sighting the lanky plain girl who was Goodheart's daughter amongst the other females, Abilene decided to seize the chance which had come his way. He approached the women thinking as he did so that they surely reminded him of a flock of hens. There was a pecking order in the group. And each member knew her place. The girl's ma, the head hen, was thankfully missing.

Taking a startled Jane Goodheart around the waist Abilene forcefully steered her away from the rest of the 'hens'. He knew there would not be much time to convey his message.

'You can't rely on Jubal Strike, Miz Jane,' he hissed.

The words worked wonders. Jane Goodheart ceased struggling.

The women, Abilene could hear, were running to their menfolk for help.

'If you want to get out you've got to help yourself, Miz Jane. There ain't no other way. Only a desperate woman can manage what I have in mind.'

'Tell me!' she rejoined.

Jubal heard the commotion which broke out amongst the women. And he heard the name Abilene mentioned. A worried man, Jubal followed on hard at the heels of Goodheart and his elders. Never had Jubal missed his Peacemaker as he did now.

'I ain't got no choice, Miz Jane.' Abilene spotted the elders approaching. He pulled Jane Goodheart towards him and kissed her soundly.

∗

Two of the elders grabbed Abilene, hauling him bodily away from a stunned Jane Goodheart. Jane, as she had been told, raced for home. She'd been warned not to look back. And she did not. But the sounds of the beating being administered were loud and clear enough to set her sobbing.

'Call 'em off, Goodheart. Call 'em off,' Jubal hollered.

'He's your friend!' Goodheart waited for Strike to join the fray. Brother Robert would know what to do. A stomping soundly administered could be the end of Jubal Strike.

Jubal moved but he did not act as Goodheart had anticipated. Jubal launched himself at Brother Simon, who was standing fairly near. Jubal's brawny arm clamped itself around the throat of Simon.

'Call 'em off,' Jubal rasped, 'or so help me you're gonna have one brother less.'

Goodheart hesitated. Briefly. If he did nothing and allowed Strike to crush Simon's windpipe, and Strike was capable of it, then Goodheart knew he'd begin to lose the support of the brothers and elders.

'Enough!' Goodheart yelled. 'Enough! The man has learnt his lesson.' And then Goodheart set about hauling the elders from Abilene.

Abilene came to his knees. Blood trickling down his forehead obscured his vision. He hurt bad.

'Get out of my town. If you show your face here again you'll be killed. Do you hear me?'

Abilene made a sound, more of a moan than a response.

'Can you travel?' Jubal asked.

Abilene lurched to his feet.

'You men,' Goodheart beckoned the drovers,

'Take this molester of women, take him with you to Obsborne.'

'I only wanted to steal a kiss,' Abilene whined.

'Get him out of here. Get him out, I say,' cried Goodheart incensed, for the drovers were grinning.

Not so Jubal Strike. He did not believe Abilene. The slyboots was up to something. His arm still around Simon's neck Jubal watched as two of the drovers helped Abilene.

Goodheart's people were bringing Abilene's horse, Jubal saw. Jubal kept right on holding Brother Simon until the mule train had left Purewater and had vanished from view. Only then did he release Brother Simon.

Simon slumped to the ground.

'Apologies,' Jubal said. 'It was the only way to save Abilene.' He eyed Goodheart. 'Abilene ain't normally a pest.'

'Pest!' Brother Robert snorted with disgust. 'The Devil tempted him and he succumbed. If he returns he'll be dealt with.'

'As for you, Strike, you stay away from my daughter,' Goodheart ordered coldly. 'She's suffered enough. And by Sunday you'll need to have made your decision. You join us or leave. Your time has run out.'

Jubal nodded.

'You'll leave, of course,' said Andrew Goodheart. 'You're a man of violence, Strike. You have no place here. You'll leave and you'll let us be. You knew what kind of man Abilene was. You let him loose amongst our women. You are part responsible for what happened to my sister.'

Jubal shrugged. He turned away. These folk might

think they knew what kind of man Abilene was. They did not. Jubal did. And knowing what he knew caused considerable unease. But it would be impossible now to speak to Jane Goodheart.

What in tarnation had Abilene wanted with Goodheart's daughter? Maybe he'd passed word to her to be ready to move out on Sunday, or maybe not.

EIGHT

Brother Robert's broad forehead glistened with sweat. His brow was furrowed with worry and the reason for all that worrying was Jubal Strike.

Ruben Goodheart sat at Brother Robert's kitchen table. He looked long in the face. A man of deep conviction, Ruben Goodheart had simply started his own religious sect. He had felt called to do it, so he told anyone who cared to ask. At first there had been three, himself, his wife and his daughter. But others had come. In the beginning his enthusiasm had been catching. But now the community was not expanding as had been anticipated. They were simply stagnating.

'This Strike's been promising,' Brother Robert declared with suppressed fury, 'to take along any quitters who want to leave.'

'How do you know this!'

Brother Robert snorted. 'Women can never keep their mouths shut. And thank the Lord for that. My good wife overheard two of them whispering. Naturally she informed me.' Brother Robert held up a hand when Goodheart would speak. 'Now hear me out, Pastor Goodheart. You've been shying away from what needs to be done. No one asked Strike to take a hare-brained notion into his head that this woman Keeley was here. And worse than that, the man even deluded himself that the congregation knowingly shielded a monstrous killer. The man could have left. He did not. He plans to bring down the community. He intends to see the quitters to Osborne. And then he intends to return with a posse. Someone amongst the doubters will blab. You can count on it. It is simply the way of it. I've no wish to hang, Pastor Goodheart. Nor have any of the elders.'

Goodheart smiled grimly. 'I need no convincing, Robert. We have no need to kill Jubal Strike. We will simply place him in the old well. With his .45. I have no desire to inflict needless suffering on Strike. When the man realizes the hopelessness of his situation he can be relied upon to do what is necessary.'

'But—'

'Here we live by the commandments. Thou shalt not kill. We will not take Strike's life. There is a difference, you know.'

Brother Robert sighed wearily. He had heard these words before. 'As you say, Pastor Goodheart,' he agreed. 'You can leave me to take care of matters. My talents have not deserted me.'

Goodheart nodded. 'Tell me the names.'

Brother Robert shook his head. 'I don't know them all. And maybe it is best you do not know those who have turned against you. In any event what happens to Strike will serve as a warning to all.' Brother Robert paused. 'Strike's presence in town has stirred things up. Badly. Things were settling. But not now. Just his presence amongst us was enough to raise a dust-storm, so to speak.

*

Jubal Strike eyed the meeting house. He had to get inside and retrieve his weapons. Or maybe, he reflected, it might be simpler to jump one of the dour faced elders.

Jubal rubbed his chin. Time had run out. He must decide what steps he was going to take. He could not afford to make any mistakes.

It was day still. Many of Goodheart's people were not about. Goodheart's community limped along by supplying horses to the fort. And limped was the word. This place was not exactly thriving.

Today, Andrew Goodheart, Ruben's good-looking son, was not out horse-trapping. He was here, purposefully approaching Jubal. Jubal felt a frisson of unease. He sensed trouble coming his way.

'Good day, Marshal Strike.' Andrew sounded pleasant enough.

Jubal nodded. Andrew's smile did not quite reach his eyes.

'I mean to leave here,' Andrew Goodheart announced without preamble. 'And if you will have me I mean to ride along with you as far as Osborne. What do you say?'

Jubal shrugged. 'That's fine by me.' His distrust grew. He waited expectantly. And he was not disappointed.

'And the others!' Andrew Goodheart essayed.

Jubal thinned his lips. The sonofabitch was trying to trap him. 'What others?'

'I think you know what I mean.'

'Nope,' Jubal drawled laconically.

'You can trust me. I am on your side.'

'Listen son,' Jubal began but he got no further. A blow to the back of the head felled him. Semiconscious, Jubal went down.

Seizing the opportunity Andrew Goodheart viciously booted Jubal.

'That's enough. That's enough!' Brother Robert, who had pitched the rounded and smoothed stone which had felled Jubal, raced to pull Andrew from the prone lawman.

Angrily Andrew tried to shake away Brother Robert's restraining arm. 'Why the hell should you care?' The words emerged as a snarl.

'Pull yourself together man,' the older man hissed. 'Women are watching. And if you ever want to fill your pa's shoes you've got to learn to control yourself. Rage is not for us. An elder must be beyond rage.'

'Let's get the bastard to the well,' Andrew snarled resisting an urge to set about the heavier man. Old Brother Robert had been a bare-knuckle fighter in his younger days.

'Take his legs,' Brother Robert ordered as he himself took Jubal by the armpits.

Semiconscious, blood filling his eyes, Jubal was toted towards the well. From far away came Brother Robert's voice.

'By rights Strike, you ought to be dead. Truly the Devil must be taking care of his own.'

Andrew Goodheart giggled. An odd sound. 'Well he will be dead when we toss him down. The fall will do for him.'

'He's gonna be lowered,' the elder replied. 'It's your pa's order. Your pa has some mighty odd ideas from time to time. And this is one of them. We ain't to kill Strike.'

Blackness engulfed Jubal. Mercifully he knew no more.

Andrew Goodheart still protested vehemently. 'This is loco. Why not just blast his head off? Or throw him down? What difference does it make how he dies!'

'Well it makes a good deal of difference to your pa,' Brother Robert answered laconically. 'And your pa is the one running things. This community is his vision. He brought it about. And he's the one holding it all together. And I would remind you, we're not killers. We are men of peace. Let the well take care of Jubal Strike. And he is to have his .45 returned. Now, let's tote him over. If you want to argue you must take it up with your pa!'

Andrew Goodheart shrugged. Toting an unconscious Jubal Strike, the two men headed towards the disused well which lay just beyond the buildings. They made no attempt to hide what they were doing. No one challenged them. Those who saw them made a pretence of not seeing.

'This man was a meddler,' Brother Robert yelled out, quite surprising Andrew who had not expected this from the normally soft-spoken Brother Robert. 'Strike was keen to lead you astray. The man wished to destroy us. He intended to bring harm to us all.'

Brother Robert's angry words seemingly fell on deaf ears. No one responded.

'And some of you,' Brother Robert continued, 'should think yourselves lucky you're not joining Strike in the well.'

The rope to lower Jubal was already waiting beside the well.

'My pa is a hypocrite. That's what he is,' Andrew

muttered under his breath as through narrowed lids he watched Brother Robert fashioning a loop to place beneath the armpits of Strike.

'Give me hand with him,' Brother Robert ordered curtly.

Still muttering, Andrew Goodheart obeyed the command. He helped Brother Robert lift up Strike. With laborious slowness the two men carefully lowered the dangling Jubal into the depths of the well.

'Hold on to that rope, mind you now,' Brother Robert ordered, correctly reading the expression on Andrew's face. 'Don't cross your pa. You'll regret it.'

Silently Andrew continued with the lowering. The rope was thrown down in Jubal's wake. Both men then peered down into the darkness of the well.

Brother Robert rubbed his hands together with satisfaction. 'We've seen the last of Jubal Strike,' he announced with satisfaction.

'And here comes Strike's .45.' Andrew Goodheart stepped forward to intercept the weasel-featured *hombre* who had brought the weapon. 'I'll take it.'

The weapon was handed over and the other man, without a word, left pretty damn quick.

Andrew Goodheart faced Brother Robert squarely. 'I can only go along with this so far,' Andrew Goodheart declared aggressively. 'We know that bastard Strike intended bringing a whole heap of trouble down upon certain members of this congregation. Now I ain't a man to bear a grudge but nor am I a man to turn the other cheek.'

Glaring steadily at a stern-faced and silent Brother Robert, Andrew Goodheart unloaded Jubal's .45. He let the slugs fall to the dust and then contemptuously tossed the useless weapon into the well.

'Now that *is* the end of Jubal Strike,' Andrew observed with a disdainful shrug. 'Now let's get the well boarded.'

Without a word Brother Robert helped Andrew board up the well.

'Out of sight. Out of mind. Ain't that the way of it,' Andrew observed, his mood now jovial.

Both men understood that it would be a mighty long while before Jubal Strike was out of anyone's mind.

With a curt nod Brother Robert walked away. He'd always known that leaving folk afoot to die in the wilderness had been an error. This was something which, although never openly spoken of by anyone, was common knowledge. And the knowledge served to deter those who wanted to quit. In the beginning there had been a good many who had wanted to quit Pastor Goodheart. In many enthusiasm had waned. But in a few, such as the elders, resolve had strengthened.

Jane Goodheart sat in the kitchen, her resolve strengthened. As she was a woman she was forced to darn. Now she worked silently, darning her brother's socks. After they were done there were the socks which belonged to her pa.

Mrs Goodheart, who was also in the kitchen, worked at the dough. Jane didn't say a word. Her mother was a staunch believer.

'It is time you were wed,' Mrs Goodheart announced abruptly as she continued to knead pastry.

Jane gaped. She was unprepared for this development.

'Think about the unwed elders,' Mrs Goodheart continued. 'You may take your pick.'

She knows, Jane thought wildly. She's heard I wanted to leave with Jubal Strike. 'I don't want any of them,' she heard herself reply. A reply was expected.

Steadily Mrs Goodheart continued with her task. 'That's as maybe but you must choose one,' she answered calmly. 'There can be no argument about it. The matter is settled.' She did not look at her daughter. Which was just as well because an odd expression momentarily appeared before Jane was able to compose herself.

The girl continued to darn. That odd little man had been absolutely right. She had been extremely foolish to place her trust in Marshal Strike. Jubal Strike, although well intentioned, had promised to deliver her to safety but in reality fulfilling the promise was beyond his capabilities. So Abilene had argued and he had been proved absolutely correct. Like everyone else, Jane knew about the well.

Jubal's eyes opened to darkness. Stench filled his nostrils. He was lying on something soft and foul.

Slowly he came up on to his hands and knees. And there he remained, rocking slowly back and forth in the darkness. The rocking served to assure him he was all in one piece. Nothing was broken. He could move.

The mood at the dining-table was sombre. No one smiled. It would not be fitting. Jubal Strike's fate could not be lightly dismissed. By common agreement, Marshal Jubal Strike was not mentioned at all. Henceforth Strike had ceased to exist.

Jane Goodheart, as was usual, waited on the men. Silently and chewing her lower lip, she placed food before sour-faced elders. No one thanked her. Waiting was women's work after all. She might just as well have been invisible.

Leaving the men the two women withdrew to a small outer room. Mrs Goodheart had already placed two bowls of food on their table.

'I'm not hungry,' Jane declared. 'I've lost my appetite.' This was true. She wanted to vomit.

'Sulking achieves nothing,' Mrs Goodheart declared as she took up her fork.

'Let me leave here,' Jane begged.

'Not another word and lucky for you your pa can't hear you. You're to marry one of the elders. And the quicker the better. I want an end to this nonsense. A woman should heed her man. Follow that rule and you will live happily. Disobedience won't be tolerated here.'

'I'm going to bed. You can clear up yourself.'

Mrs Goodheart was upon Jane in a flash. She soundly boxed her daughter's ears. Sobbing, Jane ran from the room. And she stayed there refusing to come out when, some time much later, howls of pain were heard. Eventually the howls stopped.

Entombed in the stinking fetid well Jubal had lost track of time. He could not tell whether it was night or day. It seemed as though he had been imprisoned for an eternity. In the hot stinking darkness of the well thirst plagued him and hunger gnawed at his innards.

He did not blame anyone for his plight. Certainly not Miz Aggie. He'd been careless and they'd got the drop on him. He ought to have been expecting that Goodheart would make a move. And in a way he had been expecting something. But he had become over-confident. He thought he could deal with whatever was thrown at him.

Maybe Abilene would persuade the law to take an interest in Purewater. But if that time ever came it would be all up with Jubal Strike. A realist, Jubal recognized that before death claimed him he would be long past caring what fate befell Ruben Goodheart and his murderous henchmen.

A sound from above caught his attention. Tilting his head back against the wall Jubal peered upwards into the gloom. His ears strained. And then he heard the sound again, the scraping of boards being moved.

He was not overwhelmed with hope. Logic told him that this could only be Goodheart or one of the henchmen returned to gloat and taunt him. Maybe in their perverseness they wanted to hear him beg for his life. Jubal thinned his cracked lips. Hell could freeze over before he gave anyone that satisfaction.

Jane Goodheart had not come to the well alone. Three older women had joined her. And all four women toted guns. The balance of power had changed in Purewater.

With the help of another woman Jane pulled away one of the heavy boards. And then another. With a thud boards fell to the ground. Jane peered into the blackness.

'Marshal Strike, can you move?' she screeched.

Jubal recognized the voice of Jane Goodheart. He wondered what she was about. Wondered how it was she was able to be here at the well.

Jubal squinted upwards as his eyes endeavoured to adjust to the light.

'Yes,' he croaked. He could not tell whether she had heard or not. Now he could see the silhouette of her head framed against the sky.

'I shall let down the ladder, Marshal Strike. You must clamber up.' Her voice was shrill and loud.

Two hooks had been purposely set into the inner wall of the well. This was not the first time this well had been used in this way although previously punishment had been for a day or two at the most. Jubal Strike's case, as Jane's brother had maliciously declared, had been unique.

Securing the ladder Jane sent it snaking downwards.

When Jabel located the ladder he gripped it with desperation. It was as if he feared the ladder would be cruelly jerked from his grasp. Slowly, with great difficulty, he began climbing upwards towards the light. Sharp pains shot up his legs and across his shoulders. All manner of doubts assailed him as he made the climb.

If Miz Goodheart had not properly secured the goddamn ladder he would be liable to plunge back down again with the risk of breaking a leg or his back. He smiled grimly. That might happen in any event for the ladder was swaying alarmingly. Or maybe Goodheart and cronies were waiting topside intending to blast him once his head appeared over the rim of the goddamn well. Was this all it was, just a cruel jest? Well he'd know soon enough. Doggedly, Jubal continued his climb.

As he reached the top a stout woman gripped him beneath the armpits and hauled him out of the well.

Gasping and shaking, his legs all but giving way, Jubal collapsed. If it came to a fight here and now he knew he would be dead meat.

A canteen was thrust into his hands. With a groan he grabbed it and raised it to his lips. Tilting his head he allowed the tepid water to trickle down his parched throat. He was vaguely aware that one of the women was wildly babbling that poor Marshal Strike was in need of chicken soup.

'A gun,' he croaked trying to make them understand. 'I need a gun.'

'Of course you do,' a woman soothed. 'And here it is.'

A Peacemaker was offered and readily grabbed by Jubal who was still sagging against the wall, wildly regarding a composed Jane Goodheart.

'Your pa . . .' he croaked through cracked lips.

'Pastor Goodheart has been taken,' she responded formally and to Jubal's astonishment crossed herself.

'Taken. . . ?'

'By the Lord, Marshal Strike,' Jane Goodheart explained patiently. 'It was food poisoning, Marshal Strike. Father and the elders were cruelly struck down. And Mother as well. Some pulled through of course.'

'Now we'll get you inside, Marshal Strike,' the stout woman declared cheerfully. 'You'll need a bath and fresh clothes and my chicken soup.' She laughed. 'Perfectly safe, Marshal Strike, for I have taken some myself. And then when you are ready you can guide those of us who wish to leave to Osborne.'

A splutter emerged from Jubal Strike. He knew what this was all about.

Two of the strongest-looking women took him

under the arms and began to guide him towards the buildings. To his shame Jubal did not think he could have made it inside without their assistance. More than once during the short journey his legs buckled beneath him.

'Food poisoning,' he croaked.

'Food poisoning,' Jane Goodheart repeated firmly.

'I reckon,' Jubal agreed. He knew who was responsible. Why Abilene of course. Who else? Abilene had gambled that Jane Goodheart was desperate to escape from her pa and Purewater.

NINE

Fox refused to admit that he had been in the wrong.

'O'Banion might not have been the killer but he was a goddamn horse-thief,' Fox declared truculently. 'And now you have satisfied yourself as to the truth of the matter, I still want you out of my town.'

Jubal shrugged. 'Might not!' he challenged. 'You know damn well O'Banion is innocent. You knew it all along. And as for getting out of your two-bit town I have no reason to linger.'

Fox flushed angrily. With an effort he bit back an angry retort. There were other things upon his mind. 'What the hell happened in Purewater?' Fox demanded.

'Damned if I know,' Jubal rejoined drily. 'I was indisposed myself. And the fact is I count myself damn lucky to have escaped.'

Fox spat. He was no fool although sure as hell Jubal Strike, in springing O'Banion, had made him look an incompetent fool. Fox felt as though he were the laughing stock of the town.

'I guess we'll never known then, Strike,' Fox observed. 'Seems odd to me though that none of the

Purewater folk have tarried here in Osborne.'

'They can't be blamed for wanting to shake the dust of Osborne from their boots,' Jubal answered blandly.

Fox's face darkened at the implication of Jubal's words but he held his tongue. He truly wanted Jubal Strike gone.

'If you see the Cash brothers be sure to give them my regards.' Jubal winked. 'I can read you like a book Sheriff Fox.'

'It'll be my pleasure, Strike. My pleasure.'

Jubal turned away in disgust. Fox was a man capable of harbouring a grudge for ever and a day. And now Fox hated Jubal for what he'd done.

Today was Jubal's last day in Osborne. He intended buying his supplies and quitting the town. As he headed towards the store Jubal reflected that the day of Grandma Perkins's funeral seemed far off now.

Jubal clenched his jaw. Goddamnit, Miz Aggie had better be in Red Bute. But, as Jane Goodheart had proved, a man just could not know what a woman was liable to do.

Some things were best forgotten, Jubal decided. And that included the episode of the well. Last night he had awoken threshing and shouting and for a while there he had believed himself back in the well.

Sid and Tom Cash were as ugly as sin. Fox recognized the two hardcases as soon as they rode into town.

The pair were unmistakably brothers. They could have been twins. Although there was a year or so between them they were as like as two peas in a pod.

Both sported hooked noses. And the noses made

Fox think of an eagle's beak. Both foreheads bulged forward slightly. And the top of each bald dome-shaped head made the lawman think of boiled eggs. From what Fox called the ear-line grew straggly, greasy hair which reached down to shoulder length. And to cap it all both men sported mean little eyes.

The pair had dismounted in front of the saloon and were vigorously slapping the trail dust from their duds with filthy, travel-worn hats. Even from a distance, as he approached, Fox's nostrils picked up the foul stench emanating from the two of them.

Fox assumed a smile. 'Howdy there, gents,' he declared genially. His greeting was not returned. He had not expected it would be. These two polecats were not the sociable kind. 'I believe you two gents are seeking Jubal Strike,' Fox continued amicably.

'What if we are?' The response was surlily delivered.

'Well he ain't here,' Fox rejoined, still taking care to maintain the same easy manner. 'The sonofabitch lit out yesterday for Red Bute Pass.' Fox paused to let the words sink in. 'And if Jubal don't find what he's seeking in Red Bute he's liable to take off the Lord knows where.'

'How do we know you ain't lying? Why are you telling us this?' Sid, the elder of the two, snarled mistrustfully.

Fox shrugged dismissively. 'Ask anyone in town. They'll tell you the same tale. Jubal Strike made no secret of his destination. He wasn't a worried man neither and said if you two showed up to give you his regards. He also said you were a pair of no-account bums.' His words achieved the desired effect. A stream of profanities poured from the mouths of the unsavoury pair. Fox noted that the mouths lacked a good many teeth.

'I'll skin the bastard,' Tom finally snarled.

'And as to why I'm telling you this,' Fox smiled, 'why that's clear enough. I'm a lawman. It's my duty to look after this town. I don't want you two *hombres* to linger unnecessarily. But whether you stay around or head on out well, that ain't my concern. You must decide for yourselves. You've been told of the situation.'

And with that, Fox did the hardest thing he'd ever done. He turned his back and walked slowly away from the two renegades. He knew the bastards were loco enough to shoot him. But he was gambling that, for now, the polecats aimed to keep out of trouble. The only trouble they'd be wanting was with Jubal Strike.

Sid scratched his bald head. His filthy black nails left red lines on his shining pate. There was a decision to be made here and Sid as the elder had to make it.

'We'll eat,' Sid declared. 'And take a hot soak, get the aches out of our old bones and then we'll head on out after Strike. We ain't going to overnight in this dump. I'm hungry for Strike and I can't wait.'

'But the horses are done,' Tom grizzled.

'We'll trade them in for fresh.' Sid dismissed the objection with a wave of his hand. 'The ladies can wait. We'll find us each a woman in Red Bute after we've dispatched Strike. And his dispatching is going to be long and hard. He'll wish himself dead a thousand times before he is.' Sid guffawed loudly.

Abilene's wife, the one time Miz Elisa Coombs,

came along the sidewalk in time to see the two men disappearing into the bath-house. She, too, recognized the pair. But she did not linger. Elisa proceeded on her way for she was due at the ladies' ewing-circle. It did not occur to her that the Cash brothers might not stay around for a while.

Elisa smiled happily. Abilene could take care of them. And it would be a pleasure for he was determined to add those two distinctive heads to his collection.

Yes, she reflected, Jubal owed a good deal to Abilene. It had been Abilene who had pointed Miss Jane Goodheart in the right direction. Had it not been for her husband's foresight poor Jubal would have perished in the well.

Her thoughts raced. With herself attending to business matters the small ranch could expand and become something. And when she was sure all was well perhaps she could take a tour of Europe. If she could trust Jubal and Abilene to manage without her. Elisa sighed. It would be damn hard to concentrate on the quilting but it must be done. She would commiserate with the twittering women who would say they feared for their lives whilst the two killers were in town.

'Well she ain't here,' the grizzled lawman declared with a certain amount of glee. 'The little lady quit my town a while ago. Yes sir, she lit out with a handsome young gent calling himself Pete Smith.'

'Goddamnit!' Jubal exclaimed. 'The little vixen!'

'Vixen or not, she seemed mighty taken with the young gent. Yes sir, she had a smile on her pretty young face even though she left town decked out in black from head to toe. She'd had bad tidings, I reckon.'

Jubal snorted. Agatha Munn would now get the store and the money Munn had salted away in the bank. And doubtless young Pete Smith, who must have been carrying a torch for Aggie ever since that little hellcat had sprung him from the tumbleweed wagon, would have got his reward. Aggie would have shown her thanks right enough.

'You're looking mighty odd,' the old lawman observed knowledgeably.

'Just pass me the stone jug,' Jubal rejoined. He took the jug, raised it to his lips and drank deeply.

'It seems to me, Jubal,' the old lawman ruminated, 'you've been a goddamn fool. But don't be too hard on yourself. Every last one of us has been a fool at one time or another. And that's a fact.'

Jubal put down the jug. 'I reckon,' he agreed. There was no more to be said. He'd been beaten to the post by young Pete Smith.

'Now there ain't no fool like an old fool,' the lawman, whose name was Tony, continued. 'And you've a way to go yet, Jubal, before you can call yourself an old fool.'

'Where's this leading?' Jubal enquired. Oldsters, and that included lawmen, had a goddamn habit of rambling.

'First thing you've gotta do is pull yourself together,' Tony advised. 'Quit griping. The next thing you've gotta do is determine how you're gonna take care of those murderously inclined coupla no-goods who are dogging you. I mean Tom and Sid Cash.'

'How the hell did you know about them?'

'Big Jade told me.'

'Hell! That woman ain't here, is she?'

'She sure is. She was run out of Osborne. She's a killer, ain't she? And the men of Osborne didn't hanker after having her around. The reason being if she's blasted one galoot she's liable to do it again.'

Jubal shrugged. He was not interested in big Jade.

'Now sit yourself down. Finish the jug and think on how you're gonna set about resolving your problems.'

Jubal sat down. The stone jug looked mighty appealing, given his circumstances.

'An acquaintance of mine may be able to take care of them,' Jubal volunteered. He thinned his lips. 'By unusual means.'

Tony snorted. 'Goddamn it, Jubal Strike. You're long enough in the tooth to know a man can't rely on acquaintances or friends neither.'

'So what do you suggest?' Jubal took a long swallow. The fiery liquid burned his throat some.

'I suggest you get yourself down to the livery barn. I suggest you rent yourself a space up in old Toby's hayloft. And I suggest you keep vigil. Sooner or later them plug-uglies will arrive. And even plug-uglies like the Cash brothers know enough to know they need well-rested, well-fed horses. And I suggest that when those jailbirds enter the livery stable you blast them forthwith. Toby will make damn sure he ain't in your line of fire.'

'I ain't never downed a man in cold blood,' Jubal protested.

Tony snorted. 'It's time. you started.' He winked. 'It doesn't pay to be too honest, Jubal. A man ought to have a few tricks up his sleeve.'

'I have a reputation as an honest man,' Jubal argued.

'Now, Jubal, don't be a fool,' Tony rejoined. 'What good is your reputation if you are dead and planted? If only half of what I've heard about these two jaspers is true, then they are pure poison.'

Jubal stared down at the now empty stone jug. He tried to think along the same lines as the Cash brothers. He decided the hardcases would not challenge him to an outright shoot-out. They'd want him dead but not quickly. The brothers would aim to get the jump on him. Both were sly and cunning and total loons.

Tony, who'd been staring at Jubal with outright exasperation, spoke up again. 'It stands to reason Strike, that if these two galoots show up in Red Bute they're here for you. There ain't no other reason for them to head this way. Lord man, I ain't advising you to hunt the varmints down. I'm merely advising that you stay put and await developments. You'll be a damn fool if you let those skunks choose the time and place to jump on you.'

Jubal thinned his lips. He could clearly recall those bulging mad eyes sported by the insane hardcases and the foul threats that had spilled from between yellowed teeth. Jubal did not doubt those threats were promises of what was going to happen should the pair ever see the light of day again.

Tony was right about not relying on Abilene. Abilene would do his darnedest if opportunity arose but there were too many buts.

Jubal made his decision. 'I'll wait awhile,' he declared. 'You're right. I need to have matters settled before I move on.'

'Thank the Lord you've seen sense,' Tony declared. And then he surprised Jubal by winking broadly. 'She's some woman ain't she?' the old lawman declared.

'Miz Aggie!' Jubal was shocked.

Tony snorted. 'I'm talking about a real woman, Jubal. It's big Jade I'm referring to. If it's a woman you're after why not try big Jade?'

Jubal shook his head.

'Now Jubal,' Tony admonished, 'you sure don't compare favourably to young Pete Smith. Miz Aggie acted mighty pleased to see him.'

'Big Jade is a dangerous woman,' Jubal answered.

'And all the more attractive for it,' Tony declared.

'The men of Osborne didn't think so,' Jubal observed warningly.

'All the more fool them,' Tony rejoined. 'It's time you lived dangerously, Jubal.'

Jubal shrugged. 'Maybe.'

'Now there ain't no maybe about it, Jubal. Now get the hell out of my office. I've given you enough good advice and if you don't take it you're one crazy cuss.'

Jubal grinned. 'You ain't the first to say so.'

'Well let's hope I ain't the last.' Tony was determined upon the last word.

Jake Day absent-mindedly chewed a straw. Jubal Strike was in his thoughts. Jake didn't know what the hell was going on. The latest word he'd heard about Strike was that the ex-lawman had decided to join a crazy religious community, folk who shunned contact with outsiders, so the drifter who had come enquiring for work had said.

Jake's foreman, a practically inclined *hombre*, had summed up the situation.

'If Strike's joined a commune, which I don't believe for an instant, then you ain't got nothing to worry about. If he ain't and you move against his ranch there will be blood spilled on his return. Strike's kind don't run. That's what I think.'

Jake Day had cussed long and hard. 'You ain't paid to think.' He had vented his ire on the foreman. 'You're paid to do what I decide needs to be done. There's a bonus, naturally.'

'Keep your blood money,' his foreman had told him. 'I'm a respectable man. I ain't one for walking a crooked path.'

'Then get the hell off my ranch,' Jake Day had hollered.

'My hide is worth more than any bonus you might offer.'

'Don't come back. I ain't got any use for yellow-bellies.'

The foreman had nodded. 'You can send what you owe me into town. I aim to stay around a while. I'm curious to see how this matter ends.'

'Do what you damn well please. But don't make the mistake of hiring out with Strike,' Jake had warned.

Now Jake chewed on his straw. He could justify the move against Jubal's ranch by claiming Jubal's two men had been branding J.D calves. It was plain to see that Jubal Strike was a fool. No one with sense left a working ranch to be run by hirelings. Jake had every right to run off the two thieving cowpokes Strike had left in charge. In any event, Buffalo Plains did not even merit its own lawman. There was no one to hold him to account. And there was no damn need to justify the running off of Strike's hirelings and burning the place to the ground.

Ruben Goodheart believed he had been spared for a purpose. And that purpose was the destruction of Jubal Strike.

Now Ruben knew for sure that Jubal Strike had been the Devil's own instrument. Strike had ensnared Ruben's own daughter. Child had been turned against father. The girl had poisoned her own kin and the elders. And Ruben knew it had been Strike who had passed the poison to Jane.

Whatever it was had worked havoc. Andrew, his son, was dead. And so were the elders, save three. Ruben's wife amazingly had been spared. The others had died writhing as pain had twisted their innards.

A few good people had stayed and tried to help. But the rest had packed up and moved out, following in the wake of Jubal Strike and the band of quitters. The weakest amongst them. And then, when the crisis was over, those who had been meant to survive being out of danger, the sole remaining members of Ruben's flock has left also.

One of the surviving elders, Brother John, had also elected to leave Ruben.

'There'll be talk,' John had warned. 'Sooner or later investigators are gonna show up. I am heading for Canada, Pastor Goodheart. This is a sign. A sign I am meant to leave. And I would advise you to forget about finding your daughter. Lose yourself man. It is the only way.'

'My daughter is dead,' Ruben had replied. 'And you John, must do what your conscience dictates. As for myself there is one task yet to be accomplished.'

And that task was the destruction of Jubal Strike.

'The Devil sent Jubal Strike to Purewater,' Ruben had continued. 'Strike is the Devil's instrument. He has destroyed the godly.'

'Well that isn't exactly so, Pastor Goodheart,' Brother John's wife had piped up. 'It was his quest for Mrs Munns, Agatha, which brought Jubal here. Why I do declare Marshal Strike is carrying a torch for that young lady.' And the foolish woman had twittered on, refusing to be hushed, declaring certain folk owed gratitude to those who had nursed them in their hour of need and she had certainly done that.

Brother John had stood silent. Once he would have silenced his foolish wife.

Ruben Goodheart, together with his faithful wife and the two elders, Brother Mark and Brother Peter, had packed up and left the now deserted settlement of Purewater. The small party had made its way slowly towards the town of Osborne.

Goodheart and Mark, who were known in town, had made camp some distance from Osborne whilst Peter had ridden into town to scout around and learn what he could concerning Jubal Strike. That Strike might see Peter and recognize him was a risk the stalwart man was prepared to take.

Ruben Goodheart waited for news. He was a stricken man, clinging to his faith, although his faith was rapidly slipping away from him. Jubal Strike had done that to him. He would not be at peace until Strike was dead.

Brother Peter returned, smiling broadly. It had been easy enough to discover where Strike was heading.

'Would you believe it, Pastor Goodheart,' Peter declared, 'Jubal Strike is still in search of Miss Agatha. He believes her to be at Red Bute Pass and that is where he is now headed.'

Pastor Ruben Goodheart could not help himself. Loudly and fervently he cursed the name of Agatha Mann née Keeley. He wished he had strangled her when he had been given the opportunity. Jubal Strike might be the Devil's instrument but it was that foolish young woman who had put Jubal on the path which had led him to Purewater.

Finally Goodheart fell silent.

It was Mrs Goodheart who broke the silence. 'We shall pray for forgiveness and guidance,' she declared. 'And then we will follow Jubal Strike to Red Bute Pass.'

Tom and Sid Cash rode towards Red Bute Pass. Tom was in ill humour and he made his feelings known.

In Tom's opinion Strike could wait a while longer. Tom was put out that they had not stayed around Osborne long enough to avail themselves of female companionship. Tom wanted a woman and he wanted one badly.

Pretty soon Sid was sick of listening to his brother gripe and whine.

First off Sid tried to reason. 'Someone else could get at Strike first,' he pointed out patiently. 'Strike ain't the man he used to be. He's gone crazy. Upped and joined a bunch of loons who'd cut themselves off from decent folk. And he would have been there still if illness hadn't stricken the lot of them.'

Tom had still continued to grizzle, seemingly not hearing a word of reason.

'And the bath-house gent confirms that Strike has gone chasing off to Red Bute in pursuit of a particular woman answering to the name of Aggie,' Sid continued.

'Which proves he ain't as crazy as you think,' Tom had retorted.

'It proves he ain't thinking straight. And it proves he's gone soft. We ain't the only ones after his hide and I ain't having someone else get him first.'

Sid tried to shut his ears to the sound of his griping brother. He tried listing to himself all the things he aimed to do to Strike when he got hold of the ex-lawman. It helped some but his concentration slipped and he was ill prepared when his horse went down beneath him. But he acted instinctively and escaped being crushed by a fraction of a second.

'Goddamnit!' Tom showed little concern for his brother's near miss. 'That goddamn stinking ostler has palmed us off with a dude. That nag ain't worth even a dime. When we've dealt with Strike we'll see about reimbursement.'

Sid Cash drew his gun. He glared at the thrashing horse. With a curse he put a bullet into its head. He kept right on cursing. Of necessity they must ride double. They would lose time now. Strike might yet slip away.

TEN

Sid Cash shielded his red-rimmed eyes. He squinted against the sun. 'We've got company,' he observed.

Tom was also squinting. 'And one of them is a woman,' he observed hoarsely.

'And a pack horse,' Sid was more interested in the pack horse than the female. 'We're low on victuals and the water has damn near gone.'

'I ain't stupid. I know what's gotta be done,' Tom rejoined.

'Well I know you ain't gone soft.' Sid was not prepared to concede on the subject of Tom's stupidity.

'I want first go with the woman!' Tom was drooling.

Sid gave a feral grin. 'Well just make sure you don't blast her by mistake,' he advised.

'I said I ain't stupid.' Tom was ready to launch himself at his sneering older brother.

'Then you'll know to let them get close enough before we blast them to hell.' Sid was determined on the last word.

But Tom's eyes were fixed on the approaching woman. 'Lordy, she sure is a size,' he observed with relish. 'It's a wonder that old nag's legs ain't buckled.'

Sid assumed a grin. On foot he startled forward to greet the new arrivals. He kept his left leg stuck out and as stiff as a post as he assumed the hobbling gait which had served him well in past times.

'Howdy there, strangers. Me and my brother, we're headed for Red Bute but have been struck down by misfortune.' He shook his head. 'My nag upped and collapsed under me. It happens.'

No one responded.

Sid kept right on grinning. 'We're in a bad way and mighty glad to see you.'

Ruben Goodheart tightened his grip on his rifle. 'I am sure you are.' His muscles tensed in anticipation. Fortunately he would not be shooting into the sun.

'We mean no harm,' Sid was quick to assure him, sensing there was something odd about this cuss. 'If you can spare a canteen we'd be grateful,' Sid grovelled, 'If not, well, the Lord will provide.'

Goodheart raised his rifle, one swift motion which took all by surprise. Even his own people were not expecting this response to a call for help. Ruben blasted Sid's head off and took out Tom with a shot to the chest.

'Pastor Goodheart!'

'Why, Pastor, why?'

Goodheart rounded on the two men. 'Have you learnt nothing? Men such as these cannot be taken at face value. Look at them. Can such men be trusted? I think not.'

'One of them is still alive,' Brother Peter croaked.

'Then I must end his torment.' Goodheart callously put a slug in Tom's head.

'You've murdered them,' Peter accused.

'I did what was necessary. It could be we who were now lying dead in the dust. My conscience is clear. Tonight we can hold a prayer meeting and pray for their departed souls. Now that's enough of the matter.'

'Indeed it is,' Brother Peter raised his rifle. 'This is where we part company, Pastor Goodheart. I am sorry but I cannot ride with you.'

'I have no intention of trying to kill you.' Goodheart was shocked.

'Nevertheless I will keep you covered until you are out of range.'

'What about you, Brother Mark?'

Brother Mark shook his head. That was answer enough.

'Come, wife.' Goodheart, leading the pack horse, started forward.

Mrs Goodheart opened her mouth and then shut it again. Her face was swollen and red.

'You can come with us,' Brother Peter offered. 'We will see you safe to another town.'

Mrs Goodheart shook her head. Dutifully she started after her husband. Ruben Goodheart had ridden on without even waiting to see if she intended to follow. Her compliance was a foregone conclusion.

Scratching vigorously under her armpits Big Jade came out of the saloon. It was early morning and she was still half asleep, with black hair tangled and uncombed. Yawning, she rubbed still bleary eyes.

She'd spent last night with Tony and the veteran lawman had worn her out with his staying power. He was still up in her room snoring soundly. She smiled fondly. He'd told her she was one hell of a woman.

Abruptly her smile vanished. Unless her eyes were deceiving her, there riding into Red Bute was the lunatic pastor Ruben Goodheart and his fat wife. The pair looked in a sorry state but not as bad as the horses which had clearly been ridden to exhaustion. Or maybe Pastor Goodheart's wife was in the same state as the horses, for the huge woman looked ready to topple any moment now.

Both Goodhearts, as if aware of her open-mouthed stare, turned dust-covered faces in her direction.

'Harlot!' Goodheart croaked.

'You ain't improved none, Pastor Goodheart,' Jade rejoined loudly. Grinning, she whipped up her skirts to reveal fat bare legs. And then hooted with laughter as Goodheart tried to force a greater speed out of his tired nag.

Then she remembered Jubal Strike. The ex-lawman was still holed up at the livery barn, awaiting the arrival of the Cash brothers.

Jade also remembered that there'd been talk in town of how Jubal had been dumped in an unused well and left to rot by order of Pastor Goodheart. And Jubal would be there yet if Miss Jane Goodheart hadn't seen fit to rescue him.

Jade had fond memories of Jubal Strike. He hadn't paid her a visit at the saloon but she'd made it her business to seek him out at the livery barn. 'You need a real woman, Jubal,' she'd said. 'Not a memory.' And he hadn't exactly fought her off and afterwards he'd agreed he wouldn't be thinking of Miz Aggie.

Cursing, Jade hurried back inside the saloon to

arouse Tony. Goodheart was clearly hunting for Strike.

At the livery barn Jubal was awake. He took a long deep drink of water. The hay loft was damn hot and damn uncomfortable. He smiled drily, not that big Jade had been deterred. She'd been determined. So what could he do but go along with her wishes. And she'd been damned right. He'd stopped thinking about Aggie whilst incarcerated in that damn hay-loft.

He sighed. He'd done all the waiting around he was going to do. Today, after a darn good breakfast, he was heading for home. He was going back to take care of his ranch which was something he ought to have done all along. Tony's idea had been loco. Hell, while he'd been holed up waiting for the Cash brothers, Jake Day might have been getting ideas. Ideas concerning Jubal's ranch.

Jubal might not have Miz Aggie's gratitude to look forward to but life as a ranching man awaited him.

Goddamnit, unless he raised the money to pay Abilene what was owed he'd have two partners, Abilene and Elisa. And those two put him in mind of two rattlesnakes. It would be hard to determine when those snakes aimed to strike. And whose fault was that? Why Miz Aggie's of course. He could almost hear her now. 'Shame on you, Jubal Strike. You brought your troubles upon yourself,' she would declare.

The sound of horses beyond the livery-barn door alerted Jubal to new arrivals. Bellying down, he watched the livery barn door, thinking that if the two Cash brothers were to appear he was now in a frame of mind to blast them without hesitation.

Creaking loudly the doors swung open. The ostler, Tony's kin, preceded the new arrivals. Jubal was so stunned by the sight below he could have cussed aloud, for – lo and behold – there was Ruben Goodheart. Oddly, Jubal had never expected to set eyes on Ruben Goodheart again. And Goodheart's obese wife was there as well.

'You look plumb tuckered out,' the oldster gabbled, 'but I reckon a good sleep, a good meal and a long hot soak will set you both to rights. Let me help you down ma'am.'

By way of response Mrs Goodheart gave a grunt and promptly collapsed over the saddle horn.

'Whoa.' The ostler made a grab for the reins. 'Get her feet out man, get them out of the goddamn stirrups pretty damn quick before she topples.'

'I'll not have profanity,' Goodheart roared.

'Get her down, you jackass. Get her down. Can't you see we need the goddamn doc? Lord, look at the colour of her!'

Jubal watched the scene below. His first impulse had been to jump down and render assistance. And then he remembered his incarceration in the well. If it had been left to Goodheart he would have been stinking meat in the bottom of that well. Jubal stayed put.

Goodheart was moving now, moving to free his wife's boots from the stirrups. Supporting her huge bulk he lowered her to the ground.

Cursing, Toby got the horses into their stalls. 'She's in a bad way, stranger. The fact is she looks dead!' he declared.

Goodheart, kneeling beside his wife, prayed loudly.

Toby knelt and examined Mrs Goodheart. 'There ain't no need for prayer,' he observed. 'Her heart ain't beating. It's just given up.'

Goodheart's prayers grew louder.

It was then that Tony arrived, followed by big Jade and the doc. Tony's gun was drawn.

'Lord, this woman's been run into the ground,' the ostler accused. 'Why the hell couldn't you have put her on the stage? You ought to have had more sense man.'

Ruben Goodheart sprang to his feet. Before anyone realized what he was about he struck the old ostler full in the mouth. Blood spurted as old Toby reeled back. Goodheart drew back his boot. Intention plain.

What happened next plumb took Jubal by surprise. The sheriff, without warning, blasted Goodheart through the head.

'The man was crazed,' Tony declared, shaking his head in disbelief. 'Old Toby here won't survive no stomping. I don't aim to have his kind running loose in my town.'

'I ain't much older than you, Tony!' Old Toby took exception.

'One day, Sheriff, you'll go too far.' With a snort of disgust the doctor left, muttering that he was not needed.

'I've heard that before,' Tony declared. 'Come on down, Jubal.'

'And how about a thank you kindly!' Big Jade winked.

'You've got one less varmint to worry about,' Tony continued cheerfully. 'Jade reckons Pastor Goodheart was here for you.'

'Is that why you shot him?' Jubal essayed, thinking that the affable Tony was as ruthless as any of the hired killers who roamed the frontier.

'Hell no,' Tony replied. 'This is a law-abiding town. Every now and again it don't hurt to remind folk I don't care to see the law broken. Next time a hothead thinks about jumping bones maybe he'll stop and think of the consequences. You have your way, Jubal. I have mine.'

'And I reckon you owe us all a damn good breakfast,' Jade observed. As she was speaking she was, quite unabashed, rifling through Goodheart's pockets. Tony watched with an indulgent eye, Jubal noted, wondering whether the old fool was carrying a torch for Jade.

Jubal nodded. 'Fair enough. And after we've ate I'm pulling out. I aim to backtrack a while. I won't rest easy until I know where those Cash brothers are at.'

'Keep your eyes peeled,' Tony advised. 'The Lord help you if those varmints get the jump on you.'

Jubal nodded. 'Who'd have thought it would have been Goodheart who showed up,' he observed.

'Well you ought to have thought it,' Jade snapped. 'Things went sour in Purewater, Jubal Strike, and you were responsible.'

'I ain't responsible for what happened in Purewater,' Jubal protested.

'Goodheart thought you were. And you ought to have known it,' Jade rejoined. 'You're getting careless, Jubal. And carelessness is liable to get you killed. There won't always be a woman around to save your hide.'

Jubal admitted defeat. 'Let's get breakfast! After

we've helped get the bodies to the undertaker.' He smiled mirthlessly. 'I'll leave it to another day to say a few words over the Goodhearts.'

Tony grinned. 'I'll be happy to oblige.'

ELEVEN

Jubal limped into the small town of Dry Creek. He had been obliged to dismount and walk the last part of the way as his horse had thrown a shoe. It had not taken him long to realize his boots appeared to be shrinking, either that or his feet were growing. In any event he had arrived at Dry Creek with blistered heels and toes and a firm conviction he'd been a damn fool.

Mrs Keeley, to his astonishment, had berated him soundly for not finding Agatha.

Her words still rang in his ears. Indeed he hadn't trusted himself to speak.

'You're a time-waster, Jubal Strike. That's what you are,' she had accused. 'If young Pete Smith could find Agatha why not you? No, you must meddle in matters which did not concern you. And poor young Zak Bellamy is dead. Agatha holds you responsible and said to tell you she held Zak in great affection.' As Jubal, speechless, had stomped off she had cried out, 'Now come back here, Jubal. There's no need to take offence at plain speaking.'

Jubal had eyed Dan Keeley. 'If you want to see me

come to Dry Springs. Sure as hell I won't be dropping by this way.' With that he had ridden out. He had not looked back. Those ungrateful females had riled him plenty.

As he limped down Main Street Jubal took note of a *hombre* leaning carelessly against a hitching post. The man was eyeing Jubal with a keen interest, which got Jubal's attention. However without pausing Jubal continued on his way towards the smithy.

He was thankful that he did not need to keep looking over his shoulder for a sighting of the Cash brothers. The remains he had found on the trail had surely belonged to those two crazy loons.

Scavengers had been at the corpses. They were not a pretty sight. Jubal had stood staring down at what had once been men and then the knowledge had hit him hard that he must have Goodheart of all people to thank for killing the Cash brothers. This time the hardcases had gotten their just deserts.

He knew it was them sure enough. He could recall when he'd been toting them to the penitentiary. Clearly he remembered those two bone necklaces the two had sported, human bones that is, finger-bones in particular.

From the evidence he'd found with the corpses the two had been fashioning themselves new necklaces. There'd been two thin strips of leather and a collection of relatively fresh human finger-bones. Clearly the two had been killing again. Jubal, upon realizing the Cash brothers were dead had felt a load fall from his shoulders.

Reaching the smithy, Jubal, with an almighty effort, ignored his feet and greeted Frank the blacksmith with a smile.

'Good day, Mr Strike.' Frank did not return the smile. He kept his face dead pan and immediately Jubal was filled with a sense of foreboding. Upon the last occasion he had spoken with the blacksmith the man had been smiling. Now clearly he did not want anyone passing to maybe get the idea he was a friend to Jubal Strike.

'So how are things at my ranch?' Jubal heard himself ask. He had not intended the question.

'I couldn't say Mr Strike,' Frank replied a mite too quickly. 'I haven't had cause to ride out that way. Will you be waiting whilst I shoe the horse?'

'Nope.' Jubal handed over the money. 'When you're finished take my horse to the livery. Say I'll be around to pick him up by and by.'

'Where will you be?' Frank enquired.

Jubal smiled grimly 'Where else but my ranch? Where else would I be!'

Frank dropped his gaze. He would not meet Jubal's eyes. 'Sure thing, Mr Strike,' he muttered, quickly turning away.

Jubal stared hard at Frank's back. Sure as hell, the man knew more than he was telling. Jubal guessed all of Dry Creek must, at the moment, know more than himself.

A name sprang instantly into Jubal's mind and that name was Jake Day.

Able, Day's former ramrod, watched as Jubal Strike headed back down Main Street. Able noted that Strike passed the bath-house without giving that establishment so much as a glance. Strike, Able reflected, had gotten wind that something was up.

As Strike entered the livery barn a young waddy rode out at speed. Indeed he narrowly missed Jubal.

Able saw the irony of the incident. Day wanted Jubal taken care of. A foot more to the right and that waddy would have trampled Jubal under and thus taken care of him.

Able knew the young cowhand. His name was Dave and he was, in Able's opinion, none too bright. Dave had not even realized that it was Jubal Strike whom he had narrowly missed riding down. Dave had been put in town by Day expressly to watch out for Strike. And Dave only knew Jubal Strike had hit town because a meddlesome spinster by the name of Miz Shirley Johnstone had taken it upon herself to seek out Day's hireling and spill the beans concerning Jubal's arrival.

Able shook his head. He was a bachelor and darn glad of it. What in tarnation had made old Miz Shirley Johnstone stick her head over the batwings of the saloon and call out for Dave? Maybe the fool woman thought she was living dangerously by so doing.

Able narrowed his eyes. Jubal Strike, freshly mounted, was emerging from the livery barn. Although Jubal must be eager to get out of Dry Creek, Able noted with approval that Jubal left at a leisurely pace.

Jake Day was in his study, cigar stuck between his lips, heels of his red boots resting on the polished wood of his desk, reflecting that life could not be looking better when the door burst open to admit the young idiot he'd left in town to watch out for Strike.

'He's back!' Dave announced. 'Jubal Strike is back in Dry Creek.'

'You saw him did you? How did he look?'

The question flummoxed Dave. He had to think. 'Tired I guess,' he muttered.

Jake nodded. 'Get over to the bunkhouse and tell Savage I need him here now. And the next time you burst in here without knocking I'll ram your teeth down your throat. Savvy?'

Cheeks reddening, Dave slunk out.

Jake Day bit down hard on his cigar. Strike's men had been beaten and run out of Dry Creek with Jake threatening to hang them for wideloopers should they return.

Having suffered a vicious beating neither man was in any condition to enquire who it was who'd supposedly seen them putting Jubal's brand on Day's cattle.

Jubal Strike could not be run out of town. Day knew that. A beating would not drive Strike out. The only way to be rid of Strike was to blast him. Smiling unpleasantly Day ground the cigar beneath the heel of his fancy boot. Jubal Strike's demise could be arranged easily enough.

Jubal could be gunned down when he reached for his iron. And wasn't it reasonable to suppose that any man when confronted with the burnt shell of his ranch house would reach first and talk later. In such a situation Jake had the right to defend his own life. No one in Dry Creek would say anything to the contrary.

Succinctly Day filled his ramrod Savage in on the situation.

Savage merely grunted.

'Pick out men we can trust,' Jake ordered. 'There'll be a bonus, naturally.'

Savage nodded. He was a man of few words and brutal deeds.

When Jubal saw what had become of his hopes and dreams a howl of rage escaped his lips. There was nothing left. And where were his men? Had they been planted?

Guilt smote him. Guilt because he'd not been around to protect them or his ranch. Goddamnit, he ought to have been here to deal personally with Jake Day.

Until he had seen the burnt shell of his ranch Jubal had felt ready to drop where he stood. Now, inexplicably, he was filled with renewed vigour. He understood that this feeling would not last. He needed sleep bad and he needed rest bad but for now he had what it took to keep going.

An eye for an eye, his grandpa had been wont to say. And now, as he recalled the advice, Jubal knew just what he aimed to do. Straightening his shoulders Jubal rode away. He did not look back.

As far as Jubal was concerned, Jake Day had declared war. And it would be a war unnoticed by the law, for Dry Creek lacked a lawman. Lawmen as Jubal knew concerned themselves with their own towns and their own territory. No one would be concerned at the killings in Dry Creek and killings there were going to be. Jake was sure to involve his crew. Which was regrettable but any waddy dumb enough to cross Jubal Strike was risking his hide.

Jubal smiled grimly. He wondered how long it would take Day to work out what the next development was going to be. Putting himself in Day's boots Jubal had a good idea what Day would be up to.

A personal call, what else, Jubal had reasoned, knowing that Day's kind needed to gloat and goad. Day would be looking to provoke Jubal into open confrontation. Sure as hell Jubal did not object to confrontation, but he stood alone and Day would be backed by a hardcase crew prepared to kill when Day snapped his fingers.

Taking himself some distance from the most direct trail to the Big D, Day's spread, to Jubal's own place, Jubal concealed himself in scrub and waited, confident that he'd guessed right.

Jake Day couldn't wait to set eyes on Strike. The damn fool would be dead before he even knew the shot was coming. There'd only been one sour note. A fool waddy had been heard to proclaim that maybe if Jubal had found religion he would not haul iron.

Savage had ordered the idiot back to the bunkhouse.

It was early days yet but Jake was beginning to feel misgivings about Savage. The ramrod had taken it upon himself to make arrangements of his own.

'I don't want thanks if I've guessed correctly,' Savage had declared. 'A wad of bills will suffice. And I aim to collect, Mr Day.' Savage had smiled. 'If I'm right,' he concluded. Day had not been fooled by the smile. The threat was there clear enough.

Day had conceded: 'If you're right you'll have earned a bonus.' He paused. 'I didn't peg you as a worrier, Savage.'

Savage had nodded. 'Nor am I. I just like to cover possibilities, that's all. Over-confidence is a dangerous trait Mr Day. I know. I've seen it first hand.'

It had been left at that, but already Jake was wondering whether or not he needed to get rid of Savage. Permanently that was.

Jubal spotted the approaching band of riders.

They were moving fast and rode bunched together, setting up a dust-cloud as they moved. Jubal thinned his lips. Jake Day had proved himself entirely predictable.

Once the band had disappeared over the horizon, Jubal confidently resumed his journey. Day was a darn fool and pretty soon he would know it. Jubal did not anticipate problems.

Jake Day's white-painted ranch shimmered in the afternoon sun. All was peaceful and the corral was empty. Jubal's hackles rose. There should have been horses out and ready for saddling up. Sure as hell Day's entire crew was not away from the spread. It looked to Jubal as though he was supposed to think the spread was deserted.

Jubal sensed a trap. And the only way to find out would be to ride on it and risk getting filled with more holes than a worn-out old bucket. He considered his dilemma. He wanted to see the Big D burn. He also wanted to stay alive. Jubal sighed regretfully. There really was not a choice to be made.

He consoled himself with the thought that he was a patient man and could await his day. It was, however, poor consolation. His plans had come to naught. He must content himself with rattling Day.

Jake Day simmered with rage. From the way Savage and the men were smirking Day felt as though they thought him a fool. Gritting his teeth he tried to appear unconcerned.

'Well there ain't no sign of Strike,' Savage observed with satisfaction and the hint of a sneer. 'I never reckoned we'd find him bawling over the ruins. He's headed for the Big D. Mark my words. Maybe we'll have him yet. Let's head on back and see whether we've caught ourselves a jack rabbit.' He guffawed contemptuously.

'Strike ain't no jack rabbit,' a hand observed. 'He ain't gonna put his head in no noose.'

Day's temper broke. He rounded on his man. 'Shut your goddamn mouth,' he roared.

'Sure thing boss.' The hand fell silent.

'Let's ride.' Day viciously dug in his spurs. At the gallop he headed back towards the Big D.

Jubal whistled while he waited. He was pretty damn sure Jake would be heading home this way. Sweat tricked between Jubal's shoulder blades, for the day was still hot.

Jubal had not exactly turned to bushwhacking. Killing from ambush was not his way. In any event he was too far distant from the trail below to hit any kind of target. All he aimed to do was let Jake know that Jubal Strike was around. He thinned his lips. This was his way of saying he was back. And unless he was mistaken the bunched band of riders coming into sight must be Day and his crew.

Jubal sighted his rifle. There was no way of identifying Day. Whistling still, Jubal squeezed the trigger, sending a bullet heading in the direction of the group below.

The sound of the shot was enough. The group scattered, some forking it out, others electing to dismount and take cover. Jubal fired again and then retreated. By the time they'd worked out he was not around he'd be long gone.

He knew just where he was headed. He was headed back to town. He'd done nothing wrong. He had no reason to hide out. If there was going to be a showdown, Dry Creek was as good a place as any.

'Yes sir, your horse is here and waiting. Frank brought him over in person.' The ostler regarded Jubal with curiosity.

'I ain't planning on leaving,' Jubal answered the unspoken question.

'I never thought it for one moment,' the ostler lied. 'There's folks asking after you,' he concluded.

'Folks?' Jubal questioned.

'Man and wife I'd say. A homely pair.'

'Goddamnit!' Jubal exclaimed. Abilene and Elisa were here in Dry Creek. He might have known it.

'They asked after your ranch,' the ostler essayed.

'And?' Jubal snapped.

'That there woman sure is persistent.' The ostler shrugged. 'I guess I let slip there ain't much of a ranch left.'

'You guess! You sonofabitch! You could have told me that when I first rode in.'

'There's some things a man needs to find out for himself,' the ostler protested.

'What's happened to my men? Are they dead and planted? The truth now you piece of crowbait!'

'Lord no. They were both alive when they quit Dry Creek. They were glad to get out alive. Day rope-dragged them and made it clear next time round they would be rope-dancing.' The man squinted at Jubal. 'Where the hell were you when you was needed?' he demanded.

The words slipped out. 'Looking for a woman.'

The ostler spat. 'You damn fool, Jubal Strike. You damn fool. A man's out looking for a woman when his ranch is torched and his men run off. I've heard some—'

'That's enough!' Jubal snapped. 'You ain't telling me something I don't already know. Now I may be a fool but I'm not fool enough to think Day ain't going to be informed I'm back in Dry Creek.'

The ostler nodded. 'There ain't none of his men around right now but I reckon the boys will be looking out for you. Some of those young cowpokes are sure eager to earn a dollar or so.'

'Well I'm heading for the hotel. I ain't lying low,' Jubal declared. He turned away. The ostler, he noted, did not wish him good luck.

Heading for the hotel Jubal did indeed spot a group of boys, twelve or thereabouts, dressed in hand-me-downs and patched pants. And he guessed they spotted him, for two of them headed hot-foot down Main Street where nags that Jubal had supposed to be farm horses were tethered.

Jubal for once did not hold his tongue. 'Judas hung himself,' he hollered after the young waddies.

'Let them be Jubal. Let them be,' a voice advised. 'The sooner this is over with, the sooner we can rebuild.'

'Elisa Coombs!' Jubal turned to confront his old boss's daughter.

'Mrs Abilene now,' she replied smugly.

'Now then Elisa, you ain't got your hands on my ranch yet,' Jubal cautioned. 'I aim to pay back my IOU. And with time to spare.'

'You must take care to stay alive then, Jubal,' she retorted. 'And I don't believe you will be able to pay back. Your ranch is burnt, your cattle are scattered, your men scared away and everyone else in this town too darn a-feared to have anything to do with you. What do you say?'

'I say it's my problem.'

'With my help we'll build that ranch into one of the best in the territory. You're a good man Jubal, but you lack vision.'

'So you say.'

'I do indeed. Now what are your plans concerning Jake Day?'

'I aim to rest up at the hotel and await his pleasure. He's bound to come calling. And just maybe I can shame him into settling this man to man. Any man who needs a crew to do his work is a yellow-belly, and so I aim to tell him.'

She shook her head. 'Just as well for you I'm here. Take care now.'

'Hold on there Elisa, what the hell. . . ?'

He failed to get a response. Without a backward glance she walked away.

Jubal glared after her. Miz Elisa was some woman. She must be, all these years married to a lunatic. And no doubt about it, Abilene must be a lunatic. His pursuits just weren't normal. But Abilene, Jubal was forced to admit, had saved Jubal's hide indirectly, and he'd also saved O'Banion. Jubal therefore felt uneasy over the matter of pronouncing judgement concerning Abilene's sanity.

Jubal stomped into the hotel. All he needed was those two for partners. Abilene maybe he could stomach. But Elisa would give neither of them peace as she set about building up the spread.

Jake Day watched the farm boys fight over the dollar he had contemptuously dropped on the ground.

'I don't like the sound of this,' a veteran waddy observed. 'Strike is making it too darn easy.'

'Shut up!' Jake snapped.

'You leave the thinking to your betters,' Savage ordered.

Jake rubbed his chin. Savage, he was sure, was going to be a problem. But Savage could wait until after Strike had been dealt with.

'He's getting long in the tooth and he ain't thinking straight,' Day assured his men. 'Now quit gabbing and mount up. Any of you who are afraid of Jubal, you're welcome to stay behind.' Expressed like that he knew none of the two-bit losers would stay.

'Just how fast is Jubal Strike?' Savage asked.

'He was good once. But I reckon he's slowed down plenty,' Day replied. 'That's why he quit the law. He must have been afraid of getting blasted.'

Savage nodded. Seeing Day's expression he kept his lips buttoned.

'Quit worrying. It'll soon be done,' Day advised. He grinned. 'I've been thinking. Strike deserves to hang. He's been rustling my beef and he tried to bushwhack me. Let's deal with him legal if we can. Let's have a trial. What do you say?'

Savage shrugged. 'A bullet is quicker but if you want to put on a show then I guess a hanging is your option.'

Jubal Strike had left the hotel by a rickety set of side stairs which led down into a garbage-infested alleyway. Anyone seeing him would think he was just another drunken bum holed up and trying to escape the searing heat. He was pretty damn sure Jake Day was on his way. He had a view of the sidewalk from the alleyway and when the sidewalk started to empty Jubal guessed Day had hit town.

Jubal heard Day and his men before he saw them. They rode past the alleyway entrance without a glance. An air of expectancy hung around the bunch. An expectancy of death. Jubal thinned his lips. It darn well wasn't going to be him!

Jake Day halted before the hotel.

'He's in there.' A stout woman stepped out. 'Holed up drunk as a skunk.'

Day ignored the woman. Miz Elisa hurried away and disappeared into one of the saloons.

'Haul him out,' Jake ordered.

Happily the men obliged, pouring into the hotel like a bunch of yapping dogs. All except Savage, who stayed put.

'I'll put the varmint's head in the noose myself,' Day declared loudly.

Jubal Strike stepped from the alleyway, rifle carelessly half-raised. 'I don't think so.'

'Strike!' Day half turned in the saddle, his hand reaching automatically for his .45.

Without hesitation Jubal blasted Jake Day out of the saddle, his shot taking Day fair and square in the chest.

'This ain't my fight. It's over!' Savage yelled frantically as he raised his arms sky high.

Jubal resisted the impulse to blast Day's ramrod. From the corner of his eye he saw movement. Able, the ex-ramrod, was kneeling over his former boss.

'Some folk never learn,' he pronounced mournfully.

'You could say that.' Jubal was trying to keep his eye on Able and on Day's crew, who were now pouring out of the hotel.

'It's over,' Jubal hollered. 'Your boss is dead.'

Before Jubal's eyes, fight drained out of the hard-cases. Without Day giving the orders most of them were unable to think for themselves.

Savage's shoulders were slumped. 'This ain't my fight, Strike. I want no part of it.'

Jubal shrugged. 'That's fine by me. What about the rest of you? Anyone fancy joining good old Jake Day in the dirt? Make a move and I'll be happy to oblige.'

'Mister, all we want to do now is take the boss home,' an old waddy announced, stepping forwards.

Jubal nodded. He lowered the muzzle of his rifle. Able was gabbing away. Momentarily Jubal gave the man his attention.

A shot rang out. Spinning round Jubal was in time to see Savage, his head a red bloody mess, pitch to the dirt. Savage's drawn rifle fell from now nerveless fingers.

'Goddamnit!' Jubal exclaimed. He had been that close to death.

'You darn fool, Jubal Strike. You darn fool,' a voice screeched.

Miz Eliza and Abilene appeared on the roof of the Last Chance saloon. It was she, not her husband, who held the smoking rifle.

'This is your last chance to make good, Jubal Strike,' she screeched. 'And what do you do? Darn near ruin things for yourself. What do you have to say?'

Slowly Jubal smiled. 'Maybe I am a darn fool,' he agreed.

'No maybe about it.'

'But leastways I'm a fool with a ranch to run and if you folk will excuse me that's what I aim to do. And if a certain Miz Aggie should show her nose in Dry Creek just tell her go whistle.' Jubal turned away. 'You folk can clear up the mess.'

Whistling, Jubal headed for the livery barn. Day and Savage might be heading for hell fire but Jubal Strike was finally heading home.